DOGWOOD

Lindsay Parnell

Published by Linen Press, Edinburgh 2013
1 Newton Farm Cottages
Miller Hill
Dalkeith
Midlothian
EH22 1SA

www.linen-press.com

A CIP catalogue record for this book is available from the British Library.

Cover photograph: © arcangel-images.com
Cover design: Louise Santa Ana / Zebedee Design, Edinburgh
Typeset in Sabon by Zebedee Design, Edinburgh
Printed and bound in Great Britain by Charlesworth Press, UK

ISBN 9780957596825

For MDH, on the twentieth anniversary
of Her death and always

Acknowledgements

Mom and Dad. Brittany and Clay. Ruby and Scout. Your love, unyielding patience, faith and positivity are my favourite words of all.

Heidi James, whose guidance I am undeserving of and relentless encouragement I am forever indebted to—because of you these girls speak together.

I owe enormous thanks to the following brilliant folks who have gifted me nothing but enthusiastic support and extraordinarily generous counsel:

Lynn Michell, Lola Boorman and Linen Press.

Cat Morris. Hudson Hornick, Stuart Bird and Ben Ashwell. Philippa Burne, Melissa Mann, Niamh Mulvey and Whitney Field. Siobhan Campbell, Vesna Goldsworthy and Paul Bailey. Inman Majors, Laurie Kutchins and Judy Good. Laura Harrington, Alexandra Loukas, Lindsay Imperia, Lindsey Auxier and Dr. Tina Douroudian. Dana Imperia and Anne Harrington. The Sze's: Maria, Marc, Luca and Jude.

And Marjorie's daughters: Brenda, Cynthia, Valerie and Mona, all my love.

There the prisoners rest together; they hear not the voice of their oppressor.

Job 3:18

Dear Job,

This morning after they gave me breakfast, this woman I used to know was strapped to a table and had a needle shoved into her arm. The man on the news said Tara Hackett died by means of lethal injection at 7:19am. I started thinking about some doctor, some man standing over her, smacking her forearm, digging for a vein and searching for the last bit of colour her body had to give. I figure they gave her the needle in her right arm, with her being right-handed. Could be wrong though, I never been executed. Can't imagine what it's like when they belt you down and start digging for a vein, digging for the only colour you got left.

Suppose I should be happy with her being dead and all. Everything was supposed to die with her but it hasn't, and it won't. Tara Hackett dying on the same day as your girl's birthday reminds me that everything's the same. That I'm still the same. Today isn't the best day to tell you certain things but I don't mean you no harm. Not sure what 25 looks like on you but I'm sure you're awful handsome. Probably real tall too. Bet your little girl is beautiful, so beautiful it hurts to look at her. It's my niece's birthday today and a woman who said she loved me is dead.

Tara Hackett got the needle because she killed a bunch of people, but she didn't kill them all at once. She did the first four real quick then waited a while before the last one. Police say all her misfortune, the path the Devil chose for her, started when she killed her three little boys. She killed her three sons with three separate pillowcases after dragging a cheese grater over their little baby stomachs and faces. She said she brought the cheese grater in from the kitchen, and that the reason she

7

did it was to make sure the babies didn't look like their daddy no more. She couldn't bear to look at them no longer—always stumbling around like little screaming, sober versions of him. She said by the time she couldn't recognise her sons' faces anymore, they weren't even crying—probably didn't even need the pillowcases but then she figured it was the decent thing to do. Tara Hackett did all this before unloading six rounds into the soft, booze-bloated flesh of their daddy. He had Satan in him, Tara Hackett had told me one time. She went on saying Satan made the babies' daddy the way he was, that Satan owned him—so the first time she got swollen he owned her and she had to marry him, give him his children, give him what belongs to him. Tara Hackett said God hates women and that's why they're all diseased and disfigured and killed all the time. But now Tara Hackett is dead and I don't like that kind of talk anymore.

Tara Hackett told me she killed the babies because they made her feel real sad and if they stuck around crying much longer she would have to swallow the barrel herself. She said that she didn't see no difference between killing somebody and letting them live. Kindest thing I ever done for anyone was kill them, Tara Hackett had said more than once. She told me she killed the boys' daddy because she was sad and was real scared that if he stuck around much longer he would make her have more babies. Which meant him poking at her more, more babies sucking on her. More babies stealing from her body. More babies taking whatever they could from her. More babies crying and more babies to kill. Then, after she told me all that, she told me she loved me, again.

Courts and doctors said it wasn't all her fault because sometimes when a woman has a baby, she can't cope right. She don't feel like she should. I think it's funny, men doctors and judges telling a woman how she should feel, how she should be after turning her insides out. Courts gave Tara Hackett life without the possibility of parole for killing three little boys and a man. But Tara Hackett didn't get the needle for that.

On my plate this morning, like every morning, was a scoop of grits and a dry biscuit and a glass of orange juice. The pulp in the juice and the weight of the grits sat on my tongue real heavy, like how I think grated baby skin would feel. They have this taste and this feeling I can't get rid of no matter how much I swallow. And all the swallowing and Tara Hackett being dead now got me thinking I should tell you things, everything that happened so you'll make sure things like that don't happen to your little girl. I'm sure you and me remember different. But truth is you was just a kid and I remember things the way they was, the way I need them to be. Suppose we don't really got a story you and me, but instead two stories that bleed together. And maybe when I'm telling you things I'll be able to stop thinking about digging for veins and what it felt like for three little boys to have those little blades drug clean across their pure skin. I'll tell you things so maybe it'll make my head quiet for a bit.

All the things that happened happened in summer. Maybe that's because folks sin in the summer months more than any other season. Sinning is easier done in the sticky months with less clothes and when the sun stays out, spitting its hot breath into the dry ground until almost midnight. The sun's never weak, not never.

Nothing much happened before Caro. Who I turned out to be started the day I first saw Caro and her sweaty face in the woods. The day Caro showed up is the day all this started —which is funny because I known Collier forever but the day Caro showed up was the first summer we started. The first summer we realized there was nothing to do but be bored. Slinking from house to house like lizards hiding under rocks to escape the stink of heat. Or like truck stop whores who bounce from one backseat to another. Our bodies moved because we made them, they did what we wanted. It was the

9

first summer we got lazy enough to start acting like the women who made us, and the first summer we started being bad. Collier's mama Donna said a Jezebel is born damned and she'll never be saved. Everything that ever happened to us happened in summer. Always.

Caro shows up the same June our Mother shatters the Willie and Waylon record on the kitchen floor because it's nothing but a cracker's gospel garbage. The June Caro shows up she's seven and I'm seven and Collier's nine. It's the June I love listening to Leave Home on the back porch after our daddy goes to bed, sitting on our Mother's lap. I'm seven and it's the first summer She accidentally burns me with Her cigarette. I wince when She blows on the raw pink flesh then kisses my neck. She apologizes through tears with a mouth that's poison slick and it's the first time I know me and Her don't have the same skin anymore. That we don't like the same types of touch and pain. I'm seven and no matter how hard I press my own flesh into Hers, we don't have the same body no more.

Seven, Seven and Nine

In the small pocket of trees hidden from Collier's mama's perch in the kitchen, Collier and Harper stride to the furthest corner of Donna's acres. Collier leads Harper by the hand to the very back of the woods then pulls the joint from behind her ear.

'My Mama don't like when we touch Her things,' Harper says.

'She got a million of em. She won't miss just one.' The dope cigarette is pinched between Collier's teeth while her small hands fumble with Tommy's confederate flag lighter. 'Sides, She sleep all day.' She flicks until her thumb is red and worn. Quick sparks ignite in flashing breaths before hiding again and the lighter cools.

'Hey,' this real skinny girl calls to them. She's standing on the broken roots of a tree trunk split during an early-morning

10

thunderstorm, and holding a half-eaten Popsicle that's melting onto her fingers. Rotting bark curls off the tree limbs like flesh scraped clean off somebody's bones. She is Harper's reflection, long hair with dark eyes and gangly limbs, colt-like, untamed. 'That's not how ya do it.'

'Bet you don't know how neither,' Collier shouts.

The girl walks to them, tonguing the last bite of her Popsicle before tossing the cherry-stained stick onto the ground. She shoves her open palm towards Collier. 'Give it here.'

'I know how to do it—seen Luce do it a million times.'

'Yeah, my Mama done it a million times,' Harper says.

'But ya didn't learn. Give it here, cmon. I'll show you right.'

'I don't give my stuff to strangers.'

'My name's Caro. Now give it here.'

'Kinda name is that?'

The girl rolls her eyes, places a hand on each hip and spits thick red saliva on the dying tree.

'Named for my daddy's mama, Carolyn Naylor. But my mama Tillie says she's just some dirty cracker, just like my daddy is—he aint dead but we pretend he is—so my mama call me Caro instead.'

'That's better than Carolyn. I like Caro.' Harper plucks the joint from Collier's lips and offers it to the girl with a Popsicle stained mouth and a sweaty face. 'I'm Harper. That there's Ann-Collier, cept don't nobody call her Ann-Collier. Just Collier.'

'My mama do sometimes.'

'Yeah, but Donna aint her real mama cause Collier didn't come outta her. Collier don't know who she came out of but we think her real mama prolly dead or somethin.'

'She better be,' Collier mumbles.

'Well I hope she dead too then.' Caro gently bites the joint and presses her lips together. A small flame ignites on her first try as she slowly lowers her head, letting the tip catch. The paper burns black and the body's knotted tail glows as she inhales,

11

her mouth making small caves beneath her cheekbones. Smoke leaks from the right corner of her mouth in a thick ribbon, its hips swaying as it rises towards the treetops then disappears. Red embers flare as she caps the lighter and inhales still. She shuts her eyes and pulls the joint from her lips, sputtering.

'You got a boyfriend taught you that?' Harper searches the treetops and sunlight for Caro's smoke but it's gone.

'Nah.' She chokes as Collier gently slaps her back. 'My daddy Dennis smoke more dope than Satan do—that's what my mama Tillie says—'

Since that day we all been drunk on each other. We shared everything too. Clothes, razors and safety pins, beds, boys, pills and secrets. But when I left the first time we all stopped sharing everything because we couldn't no more.

After the first time I left, Caro called every week and visited when she could. Phone calls slowed when she started working, and then came even less when she left for school. Caro got herself into this college that was pretty far away. But on your sixth birthday, Tillie brought you and Caro to see me. Your eyes were real glassy and dark. You looked more like Her than our daddy and you wore this dirty Mickey Mouse t-shirt that looked like it had been worn every day for a month without a wash because it probably hadn't been. Caro gave me a gift to give to you and we pretended like I'd bought it myself even though we all knew it was a lie. You tore up the paper and smiled something wonderful when you put the baseball glove on your hand. You said thanks and kissed me gentle on the mouth. Then you sat on the floor, tying up the glove's laces and letting your hands feel the leather.

Collier called the first Thursday of every month for six months then nothing for a year after—not a letter or a card or a call or a visit. Nothing. Then she shows up on my seventeenth birthday. They told me I had a guest so I waited in the visiting room by myself for twenty minutes just sitting there. Then, without saying why she didn't come, they took me back. I slept for fourteen hours straight. Tara Hackett didn't say nothing or touch me, she just let me sleep. I slept for fourteen hours with no dreams, no nightmares, no nothing. Caro called the next week and told me they wouldn't let Collier in because she had been real drunk and caused a scene and that they found a knife with a red handle in her back pocket. Caro told me after all that happened, Collier didn't leave her mama's house and cried for days and days and days. I was glad she did.

Caro is the smartest person I've ever known and Collier was the second most beautiful person I've ever known. There was always something that's been real tempting about Collier and the way she was. 'Can't blame her wild nature,' Donna used to say to everyone, but mostly Bart and the other cops. But Collier didn't have a wild nature, she just liked tempting other people and being tempted herself. Temptation is a funny thing. It crawls at your skin, making you itch for something you know is real bad for you. 'Get rid of it,' they say. 'Don't touch things that'll burn you—don't put something in your mouth if it's poison.' They say it because they never been in the garden, never tasted the apple themselves. They never spoke to the serpent like I have, and they never met Collier.

Nineteen, Nineteen and Twenty-One
Beyond the thick lot of oak trees sits a dirty blue pickup. The bass of *Hey Ladies* bumps from its busted speakers and the truck's exhaust breathes grey filth into the heat. Collier's mama's trees are so big, no matter how hard you try, your fingers don't touch when you hug them. Their bright green leaves wilt in the humid stink. Hanging limp on their fractured branches, they seem to sweat just as much as people do. Collier's mama's earth sinks into itself with its empty creek beds of jagged rocks, sticks and broken roots attached to nothing—a barren womb

exhaling dust and ash into the air. Barely anything grows, and what does has a short, dry life, except for those trees.

Walking up the hill, Harper retraces their dead trail from before. A path about a foot wide and so worn in brown earth, grass can't grow no matter how hard Collier's mama prays. Donna tried to make that path grow, every spring and summer, yelling, 'Girls, get off the path. Girls—I said get off the grass. I'll skin you alive, Ann-Collier, so stay off the damn grass already.' But Collier would just smile to herself and drag her heels through the freshly laid grass seed, skipping with lead heavy feet down the chalky trail the three girls made together.

Collier sits on the truck bed with her legs dangling off the tailgate, the soles of her shoes just short of brushing the ground. Her honeysuckle hair falls down her back and is longer than Harper remembers and she knows she remembers everything. Collier is still slender, flat chested with long, tanned limbs. She turns away from the woods and a leafless limb strikes a thin shadow down the middle of her face. Her body has the same bony and bulbous hinges as before, scarred elbows and knees— marks of a body with good use. Collier's body knows use, knows scrapping and running and sunbathing and sinning. Her body has been used because she's willed it to. Smiling, she looks how she's always looked—convicted, drunk, resurrected, raising a red plastic cup to her lips followed with a drag from a cigarette. A girl Harper has never seen before, a girl with real black hair, sits next to Collier.

Time slips from Harper's mouth in shallow breaths as she stands still on the sterile earth.

'Haaahhhpuhhhhhh,' Collier yells, stubbing the cigarette against the sole of her shoe.

Collier throws her arms around Harper's waist, lifting her off the ground. Pressing her body into Collier, she feels skin she knows almost as well as her own. Collier's summer scent is weed masked with vanilla, sweat and ditch drink, like always. They stand together on the ground, holding each other. Collier gently pushes her hips into Harper, inhaling her, until she's done.

'You look good.'

'Yeah, so do you,' Harper says, as her eyes drift from Collier and settle onto Tommy's truck. The front fender is bent, hanging off the frame at a skewed angle. The hubcaps are real rusted and the bed of the truck is littered with rotting newspapers, empty green beer bottles and old paint cans.

'You got bigger tits.'

The girl with the black hair rolls her eyes. Collier's face is painted with a wide grin.

'And for you—' Collier skips to the driver's side door and retrieves a paper bag from the front seat. Handing it to her, Collier gives her a peck on the cheek, leaving a sour stamp on her skin. 'Bit late, but Happy Birthday.'

'Yeah, thanks.'

'Nineteen.' Collier drinks from her cup until it's empty. She hands it to the girl with black hair who fills it with boxed white wine and cheap vodka. 'You been home?'

'No.'

'He'll pitch a fit—your daddy'll pitch a fit you came to me first.'

'Good, I hope he do.' The bag's weight pulls at Harper's wrist. Grasping it tighter, she holds the familiar bottleneck, feeling a pulse in her fingertips and throat. 'But he don't know I'm here.'

'You, uh—you know Denise livin in your Mama's house? She's in there pretendin she aint a piece shit.'

'I heard. Caro told me on the phone.' Harper casts her gaze into the treetops, searching for more sun and more air and more sky. 'Who's this?'

'Gina, used to go to school with Tommy.'

'Hi—'

'Yeah—I know, Ann-Collier told me. So, you let some dyke fuck you in prison or what?'

15

Collier grabs her by the throat and pushes her into the bed of the truck, thrusting Gina's skull into the metal planks one, two, three times.

'Knock that shit off,' Collier hisses, her voice barely above a whisper. She releases her neck and Gina coughs, wheezing as she sits up with pink lines of Collier's grasp already appearing on her throat. Collier is never one to raise her voice and she exhales as her lips taste the cup.

'Sorry.'

'What's at, Gina?' A smile curls at the corners of Harper's mouth.

'I said sorry.' Gina's so weak and pathetic Harper almost feels sorry for her. Almost. Collier collects people and their bodies like Harper collects words, hiding them until she's bored enough to forget them. Gina will be tossed out like the others always are. Nameless and forgotten, faceless with big tits and small waists, the way it's always been.

'You here for summer?'

'I'm staying here for a while.' She's rubbing her own neck and is a single shallow breath from tears. She won't meet Harper's eyes or smile.

'Florida didn't work out,' Collier says.

'What happen?'

'Open your gift, gone then.'

Harper opens the bag and pulls an unmarked bottle with brown liquid and a dirty plastic bag with a dozen white tablets.

'Welcome home.'

She smiles, almost means it. Three long swigs burn Harper's throat.

'You want a cup?' Gina says.

'Don't dirty one for me.'

'I'm real glad you back.' Collier's eyes are illuminated, deep, and the prettiest shade of blue there's ever been. Her face is all smile and she looks to the ground because she can't help but laugh.

'Where's Caro at? Where's she?' Harper says.

'I dunno—I aint her mama.'

'Where's she? Tell me where she is—'

'Workin I guess. She found herself other shit to do—'

'What'd you say to her? Why aint she here? I called her—she knows. Why aint she here?'

'Christ, perk up—she be round soon.' Collier's smile fades and her face eases. 'Jesus—relax. Don't cry about it.'

Harper tongues two tablets. 'Where you livin now?'

'My mama's.'

'Where you stayin then, Gina?'

'With her and Tommy.'

'Course you are. Why ya'll here? Shouldn't Tommy be practicin in Florida?'

'He don't play there no more.'

'What happen?'

Collier jams her hand into Harper's front pocket and pulls out a pack of cigarettes. She flicks the top open and plucks one from the box, her hand lingering at the seam of the pocket's stitching.

'Well,' Collier begins, the cigarette dangling from her lips, 'We went out one night in Tallahassee and there was this girl all over him. Hangin on him and rubbin on him and all that.'

'You hit her?'

'Nah—I liked Tallahassee. It was nice. He took me with him, you know? Didn't care what he did do or didn't do. I owed him.'

'You don't owe him nothin.'

'—so this girl is all over him. She's just a kid. It got late so me and Gina went home but he never came back that night. Next mornin, Tommy comes stumblin in then gets this phone call. Turns out the kid from the night before is fourteen years old and told her folks Tommy had at her. Then her folks tell the cops that some outfielder from Florida State was out drinkin and had at their little girl after he slipped her somethin.'

'Did he?'

'Did he what?'

'Did he?'

'I don't know.' Collier exhales a halo of smoke that hangs above her blonde crown. 'His business aint mine, but then he gets benched. They go and piss test him and he fails that, so he gets kicked off the team. He loses his scholarship and all that money. So guess where at lands us? They can't get rid of us, now can they? Not even you, girl.'

'He get arrested?'

'Nah, we left Tallahassee soon as he got kicked out. Dunno what happen to the girl—school paid her folks I guess. But he can't play no more. Nobody'll take him now.'

'Yeah, cause he's a fuckin piece a trash.'

'What's at?'

The heat from the bottle floods Harper's mouth and sinks into her throat, then belly. She takes the cigarette from Collier's lips and places it between her own. 'You aint half as blind as you is lazy.'

'We aint together no more.' Collier forces a smile.

'Liar.' The warmth in Harper's throat and chest spreads from her arms to her legs and back again. Her head is light and it's like her insides are hugging her, pulling her closer into herself, making her feel whole.

'You look more like your Mama then when you went in. That's your curse.'

Harper smiles because it's the easiest thing to do then flicks the spent cigarette butt against a tree. Gina's eyes are cast on the ground and Collier smiles still.

'Love ya more than all of em, Harper. I do.'

The first time Collier told me she loved me Caro was ten and I was ten and Collier was twelve. Me and Collier sat on the bench outside of Martin's Diner eating onion rings. She kept looking at me real funny and all I could think was that Caro couldn't come back from her daddy's fast enough—that things felt terrible when she wasn't around, lopsided and empty and it was so dark at night without her. Then Collier told me she loved me and if I didn't say it back she would kill herself. 'Honest,' she had told me. Hair fell in her face and hung in front of her eyes. 'Honest I will.' I said nothing and ate the last onion ring without asking if she wanted it first. I left her alone on the bench and walked home. The next day she met me at the corner of our street with the scabs on her knees picked open and bloody, and six safety pins that made an 'H' in her right forearm.

I didn't see her for two weeks after that because Donna made her go to a doctor and then wouldn't let her leave the house because she thought Collier was sick even though she wasn't. You don't have to feel sick to be sick, Tara Hackett told me once. Finally saw her the day Caro came home from her daddy's. That day, Collier skipped down the street with a bunch of cigarette burns on her hands and thighs. That day, the day they both came back to me, Collier smiled real big and said everything was okay and that I shouldn't worry or nothing because she still loved me.

The last time Caro told me she loved me and meant it, we were sitting in Tillie's car. The keys were in the ignition but the engine was silent and we were still for a long time. Then Caro said she was tired of it all. Her face and her mouth and her eyes couldn't lie to me anymore. We sat until I could see straight again then she drove me three counties over to a place I'd never been. She told me about the rules there and said it was better than prison, said that I was lucky. She said things would get easier when I stopped acting like our Mothers. Caro said it was for the best and she yelled so loud that I think she almost believed her own lies. She left me on the porch with cigarettes in my pocket and Tillie's Bible in my hands and the promise that she'd love me forever and would make sure bad things stop happening to me. She said she would do whatever

19

it took to keep me safe and that no matter what happened, it was for the best.

Nineteen, Nineteen and Twenty-One

Harper's leaning on her kneecaps, each cut with a pink gash, slithery and open. She rises from the porch stairs, wiping blood from her knees onto her palms and brands the front door as she pushes it open.

The kitchen is pristine with counters wiped fresh and the sink empty. She runs her finger along the spot where her four-year-old head met the counter for her first set of stitches. Running through her daddy's house drunk with laughter, her Mother chasing her. Headfirst, Harper caught the tiled corner of the counter. Three swallows of Her drink and six stitches later, Harper fell asleep in Her lap while She drove them home from the hospital. The car bounced from the solid yellow lines to the white, the rock of the car lulling Harper into a painless sleep. You don't see things happening when you're sleeping.

Harper's fingertips trace the worn linoleum cracking along its caulking, its crumbling and fading wound.

Ten, Ten and Twelve

The fresh spackle of the countertop sits under a layer of morning's grease, cracker crumbs, soiled napkins and cigarette butts. A cemetery of Her spent and useless things. Harper stands in the doorframe waiting for Her.

Luce shuffles into the kitchen with a bowl of chopped carrots in one hand, and a full highball in the other. A lit cigarette hangs lifeless from Her lips. Her hair falls in loose dark waves just below Her shoulders and Her face is all hard lines. A cotton eyelet dress hugs Her body. She sets the bowl onto the counter and runs Her fingertips over the frayed bottom hem of the stained frock to make sure the dress is still there, that it still hangs right. Exhausted, but with a sharp tongue and poison on Her breath, this is when She is most beautiful.

'Whatcha creepin round now for? Hungry?' The cigarette bounces when She speaks.

Harper hops onto the kitchen table, letting her bare and scarred legs hang off the edge, two feet shy of the floor.

'You hungry?' She asks again, flicking a bit of rotten carrot at Harper. Exhaling, She smiles though a veil of smoke.

'I'm real hungry.'

'Real hungry? Well good, real good, because tonight— tonight's the best dinner you ever have.' She slurs, Her tongue caught in a tangle with the tip of the cigarette. Yanking the freezer door open, ice cubes spill on the floor. She grabs a bag of frozen peas and tosses them onto the counter. Slamming the freezer, the door bounces against its frame and settles shut. She pulls a dull steak knife from the drawer closest to the sink and plunges it into the bag. Into the pot She dumps a box of chicken broth. Liquid laps over the edge and the cigarette ashes itself, its dead body falling and scattering into the soup.

'Put your brother down like I said?' She smiles, looking over Her shoulder at Harper who smiles back.

'Yep.'

'Yes, M'am.'

'What?'

She brings a wooden spoon across Harper's cheek faster than she lifts it. 'Don't say yep, like some goddam heathen—say yes, M'am.'

'Yes, M'am.'

'—you put your brother down like I ask?' She runs Her palm over Harper's face wiping Her trail away.

Harper nods. 'Yes M'am.'

'He sleepin?'

'Yes, M'am.'

'Good girl.' She hands Harper a jug of warm milk from the

counter. 'Say, Collier aint been round in sometime now.' She flicks on the radio next to the green cabinet with the busted hinges. As She turns the dial, speaking voices and songs blend together in a mess of sound.

'She got grounded.' Harper kicks her legs back and forth. Dirt falls from her flesh onto the floor, marking the space where she's been. And she can still feel the spoon—can still feel what She did.

'Drink it.' She pushes the jug to her lips. 'Now. I said drink it.'

'Don't like milk and don't gotta glass.'

'Don't care if ya like it or not, it'll make ya healthy and that and I don't wanna dirty up another cup so just drink it there out the top. Drink it.'

Harper pushes four full mouthfuls down her throat then returns the jug.

'Good girl. Now tell me what Collier done this time.'

'Dunno,' Harper says, rubbing her eye.

She smiles. 'Liar.' Leaning over the sink, She opens the window, welcoming heat to the geraniums on the sill. With dry dirt in their pots and only a few petals left, hanging near-dead crisp as sheets of paper, they beg for mercy. But She won't throw them out. She exhales and Harper coughs.

'S'wrong? Gotta cold?'

'No, M'am.'

'Sound like it—you need take care yourself now.'

The ends of Her hair hang into the soup of rotten vegetables and yellow chicken water. Harper figures She doesn't notice, but even if She did, probably wouldn't have done anything about it. She stirs.

'Can I pick a song?'

'It'll cost you.'

'How much?'

'How'd Collier get grounded?'

'Collier broke a lock on her mama's bottle cabinet again.'

She erupts into a laughter that echoes through the house. Harper laughs at the lie she told while She ashes the cigarette, Her cheekbones are so high they cast shadows on Her jaw. Her thin frame is sharp, so sharp with nothing but angles and corners: arms, shoulders, elbows, hips and even smile. She's all angles, finite lines and without curves. She is permanent.

'Now why she go and do somethin like at?' She winks. 'You part a that?'

'No, M'am.'

'Sure bout that?'

'Yes, M'am.' Lies taste sweet and lies are slick.

'You ought not lie to your Mama. You know that? Lyin to your Mama the worst sin there is. You know that?'

'Yes, M'am.'

'I'm the only Mama you got.'

'Aint lyin—'

'You allowed to be thirsty,' She says, 'there's no shame in it. Collier allowed to be thirsty too.'

'Yes, M'am.'

'Bourbon makes you tired so gin's better—gin don't make you tired, it makes you brave. Sides, only trash drink bourbon—no offense to your Mama, Harper,' Caro had said and that's when Collier told Caro to stop acting like a snob, always acting like she knew everything about everything all the time and thinking she was better than everybody else. While they argued, Harper jimmied the lock open on Collier's mama's liquor cabinet. It popped open, just like that. Barely even needed her help. Then they all took a turn with the clear pint-sized bottle they had found until Caro puked into a wicker basket of National Geographics. They wiped away Caro's sick with toilet paper and old wet wipes they found in the trash. They ran the bathroom tap into the bottle and watched an inch of the clear poison mix with water as it rose to the top. Couldn't tell a bit of difference with the water in it. No difference at all if you were just looking at it.

'Alright then, pick your song, young lady.'

Harper jumps from the table and reaches for the dial still warm from Her touch. The dial slides frantically from left to right and back again, both ways. A static buzz fills the room. Songs and voices intertwine, braiding together in a mess of noise.

'Here.' She grinds the cigarette into the countertop. Leaning over Harper's shoulders, She places Her hand on Harper's and slowly turns the dial to the right. The heat of Her palm presses into the back of Harper's hand, their veins lace together in blue green knots.

'Do it slow now—so you can hear and pick the right one.' Her breath is heavy and leaves a damp imprint on the back of Harper's neck. She sways, the swells of Her tits push into Harper's back. Harper turns the dial slowly to the right, just like Her. The needle slides through Rod Stewart, Anita Ward and Donna Summer again.

'Yeah, just like that,' She whispers taking Her hand away.

Harper settles on *53rd and 3rd* then hops back to the perch where she can best watch Her.

'Got good taste girl.' She shakes a cigarette free from its pack, lights a match, inhales as it catches, and then quickly licks Her index finger and thumb. Pinching the small flame, She extinguishes the match and tosses it into the overflowing trashcan.

'Don't that hurt?'

'Nope, not a bit—things only hurt when you let them.' She swigs from the highball and returns it to the countertop. Catching Harper's glance, She hesitates before handing it to her. Harper takes a long pull then wipes her mouth with the back of her hand. She laughs so Harper laughs too with bourbon streaming down her chin.

'Don't let your daddy catch ya listenin to this,' She takes another slug, 'it'll give him somethin else to cry bout. And stop touchin Collier's mama's things. Yall askin for trouble. Try and behave Harper, I know it's hard, but try. I like it when you bring Caro round—Caro's a good girl. You hear me?' She takes a step towards Harper, pushing the hair hanging in front of her eyes to behind her ear.

She has no visible fear. She smiles like She has this wonderful secret She's keeping from everybody. Her face doesn't show age like Collier's mama, Donna, and She doesn't like going to church like Caro's mama, Tillie, who loves Jesus more than anybody. She lets Harper steal sips from Her glass and a couple of times She's told Harper that if she was real lucky and maybe prayed harder, she'd grow up to look just like Her.

'You hear me?' She says, with one hand on Her hip and the other loosely gripping the back of Harper's neck.

'Yes, M'am.'

The front door slams. She rolls Her eyes and finishes the glass before pitching it into the sink. Leaning into Harper, She sets Her chin onto her left shoulder. 'Get outside, day's almost over. Don't be wastin no more time on me.' She plants a kiss on Harper's forehead and then temple.

The sun slinks down low, dusk bleeding from pink to blue and yellow and purple, like a fresh bruise. Harper's hair is plastered to her face and hangs in her eyes. Fireflies float along the edge of the porch, buzzing and treading together in the humidity. She catches one and its wings flutter against her skin in the softest touch she's ever known. Harper whispers its new name into her clamped fist and then frees it from her sweaty hands. Licking her palms then rubbing her ankles, she tries cleaning herself but all she's doing is passing dirt and filth from one part of her body to another. It won't ever leave her and she'll always have Her stains.

Harper listens to the two of them hating each other as

everything darkens. Job sleeps in his crib still while she sits on the back porch steps, picking at the splintered 2x4s underneath the soles of her feet.

She throws drinking glasses and empty bottles at him. One after another they collide against the porch door and crash when they meet the wall or floor. Harper doesn't know how Job sleeps through it all but he's a quiet and happy baby which is a good thing. He's safest when he's sleeping.

Screaming and cursing, She tumbles out of the house. Harper hears the rev of Her Buick as She reverses into the already broken mailbox before barreling into town. Harper prays with her eyes open, her hands apart, that one day she'll be that beautiful.

Nineteen, Nineteen and Twenty-One

Footsteps precede a thick body to the kitchen doorway. Luce's sister is older by seven years and has a different daddy. Denise's full figure is stuffed into a Staunton Braves t-shirt and loose sweatpants with the baggy crotch falling towards her knees, the elastic waistband taut underneath her gut. 'Jesus Christ.'

'Sorry, I just—I walked in, yall left, left the door open—so uh, the door's open.' Harper's mind skims the inside of her skull as she pushes bile back down.

'No—no, just surprise me is all.' Denise forces a smile, taking Harper in for a real long time, probably trying to find the courage to cry. 'Jesus, girl, you look like hell, yaint never looked more like your Mama neither.'

'Should have called I guess—'

'Naw, just surprised is all,' Denise says, setting the grocery bag onto the floor.

Harper lets Denise hug her, their fronts barely touching with an absence between their stomachs and hips. Denise steps back, letting her arms fall dead to her sides.

'Your Mama know you out?'

'No.'

'Me and your daddy could have come and got you. But we didn't have no idea when or nothin. Hadn't heard from ya in while now.'

'I know. I just, well, they change a date, moved it up a bit.'

'How's that?' Denise pulls cans of chicken broth and SpaghettiO from the paper bag on the floor then opens the cabinet next to the refrigerator. The shelves are clean like they've never been. Each can, jar and container is facing out, standing straight in its place. There isn't garbage on the countertop. Not a single piece.

'Good behavior.'

'Good girl. You talk to your daddy yet?'

'Nah, not yet.'

'You take a bus or somethin? Or Collier and Caro pick ya up?'

'Yep.'

'Well, sweetheart, which one?'

'Bus. Where's Job at?'

'Where you get money for a bus ticket? Lord, what happen? You're bleedin.' Denise runs a paper towel under the faucet and kneels onto the floor to wipe Harper's knees clean. Crumpling the pink stained towel, she throws it into the trashcan. 'Your brother at your uncle's. Daddy went pick him up this afternoon, they'll be back tonight.' She unpeels a Band-Aid and jams it onto Harper's knee. It doesn't stop the bleeding. 'How you been?'

'How I been? You wanna know how I been?'

Denise blushes then nods, lowering her eyes to the floor.

'You stayin with us then? Visitin or somethin?' Harper says.

'Yeah, been visitin.'

'How long?'

'You got lots of questions, girl.' Denise smiles with her lips pinched together. 'Funny you the one askin questions.'

'I said how long—'

'Just a bit, helpin look after Job. Hey, your daddy got himself a promotion. Got himself lots a work now. You know that?'

'Nope—he never picked up when I called.'

'He feels awful about that—but being so busy at work and with Job and church and all that—' Denise opens the refrigerator, looking away from Harper. 'When's the last time you seen your Mama?'

'Court. When's last time you seen your Sister?'

'I been real busy round here.'

'Real busy, huh?'

'Well, sweetheart—' Denise places the milk on the bottom shelf. The milk should go on the top shelf next to the orange juice and Her things. And She doesn't like when people touch Her things whether She's sleeping or not. 'I been lookin after my Sister's house, my Sister's son—'

'Her husband.'

'You ought not mouth like that. I'm tryin to help when no one else will, Harper.'

'How long since you first crawled in his bed like some fuckin stray?'

The tarnished band of Denise's wedding ring kisses the top of Harper's cheekbone on the tail end of a sting. It isn't Her touch, but it feels nice to feel someone on her skin again.

'You been to see Collier?'

Harper smiles, shuts her eyes so she can see Her smoking a cigarette over a pot of simmering chicken broth and filth.

'When you gone learn?' Denise sighs, reaching to push the hair in front of her eyes but Harper jerks away. 'Same old shit ten minutes in. Get yourself upstairs. Go and wash up before your daddy gets home. You look like sin.'

Harper's still smiling as she climbs the stairs, suppressing wet hiccups. Falling straight into her girl bed she vomits on the blankets that had been her Mama's. Harper coughs up puke through her nose and mouth. Laying on her stomach with her front pressed into the thin, soaking mattress, she shuts her eyes and falls asleep with shoes still on her feet.

'Here—it's the only thing I got—only thing worth havin. There aint no will or nothin. This all you got comin,' is what She had said that day She handed Harper the record player. That day Harper dragged it up the staircase and listened to *Rocket to Russia* on a loop for three hours. Harper played it until She burst into the room, spilling Her drink on the bed as She flung Herself in to the pleats of the sheets and screamed, 'Could listen to this one forever. Got good taste now, Harper. That's whatcha get from me and you get your name from me. Your daddy don't call you nothin. I call you your name.' She passed out minutes later, before the track finished, and Harper laid down next to Her, held Her empty left hand, humming the melody to herself until she couldn't keep her eyes open any longer—

Cotton mouthed, it takes force to swallow with swollen lips. Harper's eyes open to the blank ceiling. No longer a print of Johnny Ramone looking down on her, witnessing and encouraging sins. A small bookshelf underneath the window holds a few things Denise hasn't trashed: a box of old cassettes, a few of Caro's paperbacks, and Her turntable resting on the stack of records they had shared. Dusty, decaying girlhood.

Harper can't tell if it's the locked room or her own flesh that reeks of bile and sweat. Trash. Splatters of vomit cover the bed and floor. Hanging over the edge to grab a spit-stained pillow, her stomach knots, cramps and turns in on itself. She rolls back into bed, pushing the sick back into her bowels. The window's open and she's already sweating. The heat and the nausea swell inside her. In the summer you can never wash the humid stink off your skin. That sticky flesh lives on for months and there's nothing to do to rid yourself of it.

The last time she woke up outside of her cell, Charlie was next to her. When he leaned over to kiss her, she had puked onto the bed and his arm. She apologized then told him not to touch her for the rest of the day. Not to touch her again until she said he could. He washed her sick from his mama's sheets while she showered. He handed her a plate of scrambled eggs and three pieces of toast when she walked into his mama's kitchen.

'Naw,' she said, pushing the plate back to him, 'I'll get sick again.'

'It'll do you good. Eat.' He kissed her forehead and offered her a cup of black coffee. The chipped ceramic cup looked so small in his hand. He had well manicured nails on the top of his slender sun-kissed fingers with smooth calluses. Hands that belonged on a piano or something, not lifting bricks and digging holes. When his hand held hers, she could feel exactly what he had done that day, what he had lifted, moved, built, destroyed. She always remembers his hands. The rough skin of his knuckles and how easily he always found her.

Lying on her back, Harper closes her eyes and breathes in through her nose, out through her mouth. She thinks of Charlie then about the dusty record player and the way She looked when She slept—when She was safe. Squeezing her eyes shut, she makes sure no light can creep under her eyelids and now, her hand isn't her own. She feels the narrow slide of skin from the top of her hipbone down. Her hand isn't her own, isn't a part of her flesh—it belongs to somebody else. But she's touching nothing, there's nothing between her legs and there's nothing between her lips and his hands belong on a piano. Rolling onto her stomach, she feels only a coiled spring pressing into her thigh through the lazy give of the mattress. There's nothing because the hand still isn't her own. It has its own heat and guilt and sweat and pulse but somehow it's stagnant, weak and shy. It creeps in secret because there is nothing but Tara Hackett. All she feels is Tara Hackett. Tara Hackett's greasy fingers decorated with open blisters and the frayed, raw skin of her fingertips that rubbed into her, all those times she dug ditches in her skin. Tara Hackett's fingers left fading pink tracks that ran all the way from Harper's neck to her ankles. Tara Hackett left a map to remember where she'd already been. Tara Hackett was a glimmering creature. Tara Hackett was overfed.

Harper divorces her hand, rolls onto her back, seeing Tara Hackett's face burned onto the back of her eyelids. She snatches a pack of matches from the nightstand, drags one across the bottom of her left shoe, letting the flame burn for three Mississippis before jamming it into the fleshy inside of her left thigh. It sizzles and extinguishes itself and Tara Hackett is gone. Harper exhales. The scent of burnt flesh lingers as the doorknob struggles against the bolted lock, stalling left and then right. A full fist pounds three times on the door.

'The hell you doin in there?' Denise yells. 'Why's the door locked?'

'I lock it cause I can.'

'It's your daddy's door in your daddy's house. Now get down here. Nearly three in the afternoon and your daddy wanna talk. He in his sittin room, so cmon now.'

'What's he got a sittin room for anyhow? We don't need no sittin room,' Harper shouts into the pillow.

'Don't keep him waitin no longer.'

Harper rubs the drunk from her eyes as she walks into the kitchen. She watches Denise cracking eggs. A bit of shell falls into the bowl but she doesn't say anything.

'What you waitin for, girl?' The apron stretched around her inflated figure anchors her to the ground.

For the first time in her life, he looks old. His dark hair is cropped tight to his scalp and he's graying at his temples. His brown eyes are a shade closer to black, a shade closer to nothing. Weak. He was thin, but now he's gaunt. He's fragile and tired and hungry. His eyes and mouth are framed by creases. Half of those lines belong to Harper, and the other half are Hers. He smiles, not showing any teeth, and walks to her. He looks into her. Placing a hand on each side of her face, he brings his lips to her forehead in a dry kiss.

'Hi,' Luke says. 'Shoulda called.' His arms hang limp at his side. Harper interlocks her fingers behind his back and holds him. Kissing her again, he unlocks her grasp. 'I'd sent somebody for you if you'd said you was gettin out early. How'd you get back?' He sits behind the desk with a face full of nothing.

'Bus.' She forces both hands into her pockets because it seems an easy thing to do.

'Liar—somethin happen yesterday?' His small hands rest on the desktop next to a picture of him and his three older brothers, Harper's uncles who she's never met. One time She said there was no reason to meet her uncles, 'Rat bastards,' She had said. '—won't help nobody, not even their own family,' She had said. 'But that's what happen when you start swellin in a Red State,' She had said. Harper owns and tongues all of the things She said.

'You been runnin your mouth?'

'No.'

'You always run your mouth. You go see Collier before you come home? Aint even been out three hours—hadn't even been out three hours before you go and do somethin so goddam stupid. Sure as hell you breakin parole, aintcha?' He speaks in a voice barely above a whisper. 'What's it about sunlight that makes you sin? Then you go and run your mouth to your aunt.'

No one looks at Denise when She's around. That's how it's always been. That's why Denise hates Her daughter, because Harper's Her kind.

'Smells like sick upstairs.'

'I don't feel good. I'm sick or somethin.'

'Lie about as good as your Mama does—you need to get somethin to eat.'

'No, I aint hungry.'

'Your first word was no. You know that?' he says. 'So?'

'So what?'

'So what now?'

'Whatcha mean?'

'You retarded or drunk, Harper?'

She says nothing. His quiet, almost black eyes make his words gentle and blank, void of any meaning. You can't hear sense from a man that scared.

'Are you clean?'

'Yeah.'

'You got a parole officer?'

'Yeah—Mitch or somebody. I forget.'

'You have to test?'

'Yeah.'

'Yeah? You gone pass?'

'Yeah.'

'You been pillin with Collier?'

'I'll pass.'

'Sure bout that?'

'You heard me.'

'So, you done?'

'What?'

'Done. All this over for us? When's all this garbage over, Harper?'

'You never really done'—that's what Tara Hackett said once. She was right too. When they say you can leave, you can all right—that part is true. They fill your pockets with whatever they stole from you before, then they open the door and you just walk on out. But what they don't tell you is you never really done. Never really finish your sentence, serving your state, serving the men who keep the keys to your cell. Tara Hackett said all these things while she watched me wash my hair. 'Maybe they let you leave, but you always serving. You think just because they unlock a door you can stroll out and think you normal? Get back everything you missed? Your

sentence never really over. Not never.' Tara Hackett was right about a couple things. That's why all those men made her silent, took her voice so she couldn't keep being right about the way things are. But that's not the reason they killed her. They killed her because she went and killed a bunch of people and one of the people she killed was somebody I loved.

'Yeah, it's over—good behavior and that.'

'That so? You on good behavior?' He glares at her the way he used to when he'd come home after work, when he'd come home and find Job screaming and sitting in an eight-hour diaper. She'd be asleep next to the radiator in the basement while Caro and Harper and Collier sat in his living room guzzling bottles of cough syrup they'd swiped from Tillie's medicine cabinet.

'Yeah, I am. I said I am.'

'You wanna stay here?'

'Yeah.'

'What's that?'

'Yessir.'

'If that's a case, you help out with Job, get yourself some work or back into school. Y'understand?'

'Yeah.'

'I don't got time to sit round and babysit no more. Yaint a kid no more. Eighteen's an adult.'

'I'm nineteen.' He says nothing, so she fills the silence again. 'How's She?'

Opening the top drawer of his desk, he pulls out a pack of cigarettes. He takes one for himself and tosses a spare to Harper. 'I been real busy.' He won't look at her, just sucks on the cigarette as he lights it, probably praying the filter will never come to his lips. 'I gotta lot goin on, got lots to do to make sure She can stay and get tended like She need. You won't here for none of it when it all happen, didn't see what She did. You a lucky girl bein gone like you was. But now I pay for it, pay for that place. Pay for your Mama. Outta my pocket I pay for yall's sins.'

'I'd like to see Her.'

He says nothing and her cigarette lies still on his desk.

'You don't have to go in—I just need a ride is all.'

He places the pack back into the drawer and returns the lighter to his pocket. 'I'll think about it.'

They hesitate, each waiting for a rescue from the other to kill the silence. He never could stand the silence, can't stand the sound of his own breathing and the gaze of another person on him, taking him in and sizing him up.

'You uh, you doin okay then?' he says, leafing through a stack of papers.

'Yeah.'

'Give it a rest with Collier, will you? I'll ask round and see if we can get you a job—need you to stay outta trouble. Can't afford nothing else to happen. You hear me?'

'Where's Job at?'

'Swimmin.'

'He know I'm back? He know I'm here?'

'I should get back to work,' he says, 'but uh, glad you okay.'

'That so?' She has never seen a man suffocate himself on such simple words.

'Mind your aunt. Get some lunch, clean yourself up and stop being so goddam lazy. And Harper—'

'Yeah?'

'Shut the door, will you?'

Denise's body consumes the kitchen and Harper can barely breathe.

'Carolyn Naylor been waitin for you.'

'What? Where's she?'

'Out front—told her you was with your daddy. Have somethin to eat before you leave—before you leave again. Please.'

'I said aint hungry.'

Sitting on the front porch, Caro is the same with summer freckles, tanned June flesh and sun-bleached streaks. Tillie gave her dark hair and pale skin but summer claims Caro's body like always. She's sitting on the porch, not smoking a cigarette and her right hand looks empty without one. The door slams and Caro smiles, looking up at Harper.

'You look good,' Caro says, standing, 'but Jesus, you smell like Collier.'

Harper says nothing, wrapping her arms around Caro as tight as she can.

'You look really good.' Caro presses her lips to Harper's ear when she speaks, like Tillie used to.

Caro isn't half the liar Collier is, and Collier isn't half the liar Harper is. They have a pact to believe each other's lies. A covenant to never question each other.

'So do you.' Harper releases her.

'I called three times yesterday afternoon and then came by after work last night but Denise said you passed out. They wouldn't let me in the house.'

'They're both assholes.'

'I wish you would have let me come get you. Jesus—what happen?' Caro steadies herself with her palm on Harper's knees. She inspects the fresh, nickle-sized burn at the cuff of Harper's shorts, the kiss of three Mississippis branding the inside of her thigh. Dead skin peels back on itself, the raw edges exposing her wet flesh.

'Get off your knees, Caro.'

Caro rises slowly, staring at Harper. Staring like maybe she's searching for some piece of evidence that's on Harper's body about where she's been, what she's done, what's been done to her. Like maybe some scar, scrape or scab would tear and leak the answers to all the questions Caro wants to ask but doesn't have the courage to. Harper feels the words lodged in Caro's throat. Like Caro's throat is tightening and she can't choose which ones to cough up so she can breathe again.

'How you been?' And Harper's words save them.

Caro smiles with the right side of her mouth, like there's a fish hook caught in the corner where her lips meet. Caro hugs Harper again. 'Been well.' Caro locks her arms around Harper's waist again. Holding Harper for what seems a while, but not long enough. Caro releases her. 'You hungry?'

'Starvin,' Harper says, squinting in the afternoon sun.

They walk to Tillie's car. Harper sits up front. Caro gets behind the wheel and rolls the windows down.

'Sorry, air conditioner's broken, and the seat too, so just— well, just sit pretty still and it'll be fine.'

Harper smiles, lighting a cigarette for herself and then one for Caro.

'I don't really smoke anymore—' Caro pauses before taking it and then starts the engine.

She carefully reverses out of the driveway and they say nothing as the car picks up speed. Harper slips her shoes off and places her bare feet onto the dashboard. She reclines her seat, closes her eyes, facing the window and drowning in sunlight. No matter how much, it isn't bright enough, her skin can't drink enough. There is sun everywhere on her for as long as she wants.

'Are you going to be sick?'

Even though her eyes are shut, Harper can hear the smile on Caro's face.

'Shut up.'

'You sure?'

'Already was.'

'Already was,' Caro mocks. 'Course you were.'

'When you go back?'

'To work? Tonight, round seven I think.' Caro ashes her cigarette out the window and flips on the radio. She bounces from station to station. Stuttering on *Hot Stuff* she mumbles, 'I hate Donna Summer.'

'Slit her throat if I could,' Harper says, smiling, 'I meant school. When you back to school?'

'Not till month after next.'

'Awful soon.'

'Summer's half over.'

'Summer aint never over. Whatcha studyin then?'

'History.'

'Girl, you a nerd.'

'Yep.' Caro doesn't look away from the road.

'So what? You gonna move then or what?' Harper says.

'I mean I live over there during the year. Too far to drive it every day. It's like a four hour drive each way, you know?'

Caro can't drive them fast enough through town. She whips the car around sharp bends. The roads wind crooked, hooked around Dogwood trees and along the banks of the shallow and thirsty creek beds. Everything outside of the car is a blur of blue and brown. Caro can't get them through town fast enough.

'What about when you're done, when you graduate. What then?'

'I dunno, depends I guess.'

'On what?'

'Well, if I get a job or not around there, or if I have to go somewhere else to find one.'

'Why don't you get a job here?'

'Don't say things like that, makes you sound like Collier.' Caro smiles, nudging Harper gently with her elbow. The ashes from Caro's cigarette fall onto her bare knees. 'You should come visit me in the fall, think you'd really like it.'

'Yeah, maybe.'

'You going back to school? You should.'

'I got my GED last fall.' Harper brushes the dead ashes from Caro's skin.

'Why didn't you tell us? You should have told us. We'd of come you know,' Caro says, flicking her half-smoked cigarette out of the window. 'Your folks go?'

'No.'

'You tell them about it?'

'No.'

'Why not? I'm sure they would have come if you'd told them.'

Harper takes another drag as Caro glances into the rearview mirror with the hope that there's someone in the backseat telling her what to say, '—you know better than that.'

'They ever let you out to see Her?' Caro asks.

'Nope.'

'She call?'

'Nope.'

'I uh—I saw Her—' Caro gazes blankly through the windshield. She won't meet Harper's glance and Harper can't tell if Caro is concentrating or scared or bored or something else.

'When?'

'Right after you left, then right after She left, and then on Her birthdays and your birthdays. There were other times too but, I dunno, they bleed together. I can't remember sometimes.'

'How was She? How's She?'

'Good.'

'Good? When She ever been good?'

'She didn't say much. Don't think She really wanted to see us.'

'Tillie went?'

'Course she did.'

'What She say?'

'Not much.'

'Tell me exactly what She said.'

'She uh, She wanted to know if you were out yet—if I had seen you. She said that—She said She wondered if you looked the same, wondered if you still looked like Her. She's afraid you're going to get out and not look like Her anymore. And She said She wants you to come see Her as soon as you can.'

'Bet She does.'

'You should, you know?'

'She know bout Denise?'

'Doubt it, I mean I didn't tell Her. I can drive you down

there this weekend. Can take you to see Her if you want.'

They say nothing else as they coast down the road. The stench of dead grass and stale mulch fill the car. Caro turns right into Martin's, pulling into a parking space and killing the engine. 'I'm sorry, you know? I am—'

'It's fine,' Harper says.

Caro scoffs and forces a smile. 'I know. I'm real glad you're back.' She gives Harper's hand a quick squeeze then unlocks the door. 'You can get out now, door's open.'

Four men sit at the counter, four daddies whose fleshy pale stomachs lap over their worn belts. Deep pores and broken blood vessels paint their noses, and thinning hair covers their heads. Their sweaty sunburned faces melt together in a glance towards Harper and Caro. They soak the girls in, drink them down. They watch the girls just like they used to during the other summers, when there's no choice but less modesty and more skin. Harper looks each man in the eye. Caro keeps her head low, like a dog, unable to meet their gazes and claim Harper as her own.

The twelve dirty tables are littered with the edible remains of a week's worth of unemployed men who get wasted to waste time. It reeks of fried garbage and cheap American cigars. They sit at a table set for six and Caro hands Harper a menu that is never opened. Mike Gentry walks towards them. Harper grins at Caro who mutters, 'Jesus,' and buries her face into a menu.

'Careful Caro, your mama don't like that kinda talk,' Harper says.

Mike fumbles with his own smile. The open slit of his mouth looks foreign on his face. He used to follow Caro and Harper and Collier around after school and roll a joint before they walked home. They'd raid his cabinets when his folks were out of town at the empty promise Caro would love him forever. They'd guzzle his daddy's gin then fill the deficit with water from the rusting bathroom tap.

'He's disgusting,' Caro says, with the menu covering her face. 'Be nice.'

'Hi,' Mike says, setting two glasses of water on the table. His face is the same but he's much taller than both of them now. If Harper hadn't known him, known that his daddy's crank had eaten away the raw, skinny boy muscle underneath his skin, from the neck down she would have thought he was a little girl who hasn't gotten her period yet.

Caro takes long, consecutive gulps of her water, nearly finishing the glass. She lets the water silence her. When she returns the glass to the table, it's branded with a frosted pink stamp from her bottom lip. Harper smiles at Mike, trying for her and Caro both.

The dull roar of a beaten-up engine revs in the parking lot. With a cigarette perched in the corner of her mouth, Collier jumps out and slams the driver's side door behind her. A small bell rings her entrance. The men all look at her.

'How many times I say can't smoke inside no more, Collier? I'll be back for yalls order.'

'You—now you look like shit,' Collier says, with a thin strip of her stomach teasing the room as her shirt rides up. She kisses her fingertips then presses her prints to Harper's forehead. Sitting next to Caro, she kisses her cheek and Caro flinches as Collier's skin meets her own. 'Welcome home then. Hey Caro— you uh, you sat on him since you been back from school?'

Caro says nothing but her eyes look grayer. Scowling, they lose their real pretty flecks of hazel and green.

'He aint nothin but a dickhead with a chickenshit habit.' Collier offers her cigarette to Harper who accepts it. She takes a long drag and passes it to Caro who rolls her eyes then does the same.

'Put it out Collier. You deaf?' Mike shouts, dumping a white bag into the fryer. Collier snatches the cigarette from Caro, takes a final drag and grinds the butt into the table. 'Whatcha want?'

'Grilled cheese,' Caro says, looking out the window.

'Gimme a tea.' Collier places her cigarettes and lighter on the table. 'Not type a tea you like though, sweetheart.'

'You want fries or onion rings, Caro?'

'Onion rings.' Caro picks at the darkest shade of a scab on her right elbow.'

'Don't, it'll scar. It will,' Harper says, swatting at Caro's hand. She says it because Caro had said the same thing to her more than once. And Harper figures she owes Caro the same, to save her skin from scarring. 'Stop—don't touch it.'

'Harper?'

'I'll have a same, please.'

'Fries or onion rings?'

'Said she wants same thing. And don't forget my lemon.'

'Onion rings, please,' Harper says. 'Thanks.'

'Good choice. Yesterday, Pete saw a whole family a roaches back in the potato bag.'

'What if we had ordered fries then?'

'Prolly would have told you there's roaches in the onions.' Mike winks and Harper smiles with her teeth hidden behind her lips. She watches him turn and walk into the back.

'Careful, you get in more trouble if you keep smilin like your Mama used to. Don't smile at that faggot again.'

'Jesus, shut up, Collier.'

'Aint nobody talkin to you, Carolyn. So we doin somethin tonight?'

'I can't,' Caro says.

'Why not, princess?' Collier pulls six orange tablets from her pocket. She sets two in front of each of them. Harper quickly pops hers into her mouth and Collier does the same. Caro sighs, pushing hers towards Collier who smiles and splits the pair between her own tongue and Harper's.

'I have to work.'

'You work every night then?' Harper asks.

'Have been. We're short on people. If you want some work,

they'd probably take you. Come by tonight. It's real easy there. It is.'

'Yeah, maybe.'

'Come round tonight—everybody solved they problems.' Collier slugs Harper's water.

'Besides, I have class in the mornin.'

'Thought you don't go back till next month,' Harper says.

'I have summer classes.'

'Busy girl, aintcha Carolyn?' Collier says with a smile and a wink.

And Harper watches Caro slip.

'You got heaps to say today, Ann-Collier. Where's Gina? Thought she'd be round for a while. She didn't last half as long as the others.'

Collier says nothing and Caro keeps forcing herself to smile.

'Thought that spic stay round for a while.' The words pour from Caro's mouth in deep waves. She's drowning herself, Caro's slipping into Collier and she can't catch herself. Collier's smile paints her entire face.

Collier cackles, her smile spreading wider. Her mouth leaks a sweet thick poison you can't say no to. 'Careful girl, your mama don't like that kinda talk.'

Harper says nothing while she watches Mike balance two plates of food on his outstretched right arm and a glass of iced-tea in his left hand. A ratty blue apron hangs loosely on his frame. Looking like a little boy wearing his father's clothes, his shaggy brown hair hangs over his forehead and the tops of his ears. He sets the plates and glass on the table.

'Well, that was mighty quick. Always count on you, Michael.'

He won't look at her because he's scared of her too. 'Yall need anythin else?'

'Lemon,' Collier says, still staring into Caro, still tasting her words.

'Yeah, there is.' He dries his hands on the bottom of his apron.

'Being awful stingy. Gimme some more.'

Harper's eyes settle on the back of Mike's neck as he walks towards the counter of men.

Caro takes a bite of her sandwich and Harper does the same then offers it to Collier who accepts.

'You sure you don't want to order something?'

'Yeah, I'm sure.' Collier returns the sandwich to Harper's plate and reaches onto Caro's for an onion ring. Caro smacks her hand and Collier picks an ice cube from her glass then flicks it at Caro.

'Stop. You want to order something or not?' Caro says. 'Why the hell you want to eat when you just had pills?'

'Don't talk to me like I'm a child. I don't wanna order nothin—just want one and I can't order just one, now can I?'

Mike walks back to the table and tosses a full, uncut lemon into Collier's glass, smiling at Harper.

'Fuck off, faggot—cmon Caro, gimme one.'

'No.'

'You owe me.'

'Everybody owes you something, Collier. You think everybody owes you something.'

Caro is right. Everybody owes Collier something. Collier knows she has a power over people. She always has and she can make men and women and boys and girls and even Christians do whatever she wants.

Collier lights another cigarette as she watches Mike walk back into the kitchen. She takes a long drag and ashes into the vase.

'Remember Jeremy?'

'Jesus, Me and Harper was twelve.'

'You know, Carolyn, you shouldn't take the Lord's name in vain. Can't wait to tell your mama bout the filth on your lips, the lips on your face just as filthy as the ones you hide, huh? You know what else? If I hadn't done what I did—he would have made you. So, you welcome. I saved you. Least you can do is give me an onion ring. Remember when I got sick and swollen because a him. You remember, Harper?'

'That shit was filthy,' she says, wiping the grease from her hands and watching Mike's shoulders rise and dip as he cuts and cubes potatoes next to the grill.

'Tell you what, I bet if he wasn't dead and I put an onion ring on his cock rot, you'd eat it right up.'

Caro tries to hide a smile but can't. After she takes a bite of her sandwich, she slides the plate to Collier who smiles too.

'Thank you, Carolyn.'

Caro forgives Collier with a crooked smile, three bites of a grilled cheese and four onion rings. Or maybe Collier forgives Caro. Sometimes it's hard to tell them apart.

Then Caro talks about work, about how at the bar sometimes you get groped a bit and stuff like that, but the tips are really good. Tips make everything worth it.

'Whatcha think gone happen?' Collier says. 'Everythin cost somethin.'

'But you should Harper—come by tonight, please, I'll get you some work.'

'I will.' She pushes her plate to Collier who wipes it clean.

'Then you can save up a bit of money and you come visit me in the fall. I could help you with applications and all that, you know? If you want to. Think it would do you good. You'd be good for it.'

'Sweetheart, you don't need a job or school, you just need to make sure your parts still work.'

'Christ, Collier—'

'Be nice, Carolyn. When you gone learn school's nothin but a place that takes you away from your mama's house, where your mama who raised you, needs you right now.' Caro says nothing and Harper says nothing so Collier keeps breathing. 'Harper, you need make sure your parts still work all right. That's all that matter.'

Harper meets Collier's glance briefly. She winks, takes a sip of her tea then smiles at Harper without showing any teeth.

'Yall need anythin else?' Mike calls, from behind the counter.

Michael, he who is *like God* in Hebrew.

He insisted they leave the lights on, even though the clock showed three in the morning. She wishes he hadn't. The light somehow made him even closer to invisible than he already was. She barely touched his face, afraid if her hand or lips brushed a bit too hard against his hollow cheeks, the walls of his skull would somehow crumble. He was fragile like a pet, or a baby—it disgusted her but not enough to tell the truth. She's never been good at saying no. Don't know how to. That's what a Mother is supposed to teach you.

It started with him bucking wildly, grinding his hips into hers as the junk hit him. But he wasn't there. He was lost, somewhere on his own. But she was gone too—tight at first but then she melted, tasting the drip at the back of her throat as the music swam back to her. 'I aint never been with a felon before,' slipped from his lips but she kept her eyes shut and received him, like she's supposed to. He was a rotting exoskeleton and his eyes were vacant and she wanted to vomit out her ears but she didn't know if that was because of the pills or because of something else. He was all knees and elbows and their eyes never met. He tired quickly.

His arms are sprawled across the pink sheets. If she had the right tools she would nail both his frail wrists to the bed. She would let his pulse bleed out onto his little boy hands and watch his mama's sheets stain. The thin planks of his chest rise and fall in shallow breaths. His ribs fight against his own taut skin, poking out along his sides. She wants to strip his skin clean off the bone and laugh. Skin him like the doe he is so she can cackle like a witch. Cackle like a possessed witch. Collier will laugh too. Harper knows Collier will laugh too because she loves destroying things beyond redemption.

Harper pushes herself up as the sheet falls to her waist.

Mike's wallet on the nightstand is empty except for an expired driver's license, three quarters, and some torn papers. Harper reaches into the trashcan next to the bed and pulls a crumpled pack of cigarettes from the night before. He grunts and rolls over towards the far wall.

She stands and walks to the open window, feeling the sunrise cast onto her body. Her skin is dry and pale, thirsty. She barely casts a reflection in the mirror hanging just below his mama's crucifix. Her neck is stamped in light rings of purple and yellow, bruised and dented with small impressions of his incisors. She's branded. And looking into the mirror, topless, she feels Collier.

Jenny down the hall has a smile like Collier used to have. And Jenny down the hall has a little girl just like you. Jenny has only met her little girl once because the state thought she was an unfit mother, so they snatched the little girl from her. Jenny's room is full of photos of her little girl doing things little girls should be doing—running around outside, playing with unbroken toys and using crayons in a colouring book.

Jenny has a smile like Collier used to have. There's something slow and easy about it, the way her lips curl up showing her straight teeth and I can't help but smile myself when Jenny smiles. Just like Collier, Jenny is good at smiling even when she doesn't want to. Jenny doesn't have chores in the kitchen like the rest of us because she told our house mother that being close to the knives is too strong a temptation for her, being a recovering cutter and all. 'They're dumb as rocks,' Jenny said the other day, helping me fold my laundry, 'Knives in the kitchens barely sharp enough to slice bread.' And Jenny is a real pretty girl, like Collier used to be.

She broke curfew last week and begged me to stay quiet when I saw her slip into her room and out of her dress. 'I'll do anything, please, anything. Just please don't say nothing. Really, anything, I mean it,' she said, her red eyes watering but not the type of watering that comes from crying. Jenny is a real pretty girl but she's sad. She's sad because she thinks she'll live forever. Living forever means nothing ever stops. And all Jenny wants is for everything to stop. Jenny dares God to kill her every night but I want to tell Jenny to stop sneaking out when it gets dark and getting high and I want to tell her not to worry because she won't live forever.

I can't think of nothing worse. I'm sure there's no worse thing in the whole wide world than that—living forever.

Nineteen, Nineteen and Twenty-One
Harper pops the white pill she earned into her mouth and swallows. Pacing along the fence next to the baseball field at the elementary school, she drags her shoes through the brittle brown grass and kicks at the dry earth. The ground is desperate for rain. She shuffles her feet back and forth along the path as kids fill the dugout. They laugh, throwing cups of water on each other until nine red-capped bodies scatter onto the field.

It's easy to spot him—shortly cropped hair under the red hat, with a smile that can be a bit crooked at times, just like Hers, and long limbs with dirt-caked scabs and fresh bruises, a body older than his mind. Harper and him both look nothing like their daddy. Once, Harper heard him ask Her if they were even his. Harper said nothing and just listened to Her cackle in the kitchen, listened to the smile on Her face. 'You'd love to know that, now wouldn't you, sweetheart?' She had said.

Job tosses the ball to the kid pitching and jogs to second base. He's elegant for a little boy, swift and precise in his movements. His feet shuffle quickly to position himself and he cleanly fields the ball when it's hit to him. And then, with a quick snap of his wrist, he throws ahead of the runner. He's perfect every time.

There's a small house with a backyard shed just beyond the

third base dugout. A house with a backyard shed Caro and Harper and Collier know well. The shack of many firsts has a sinking roof, a yard of rising weeds and a splintered rope hanging from a branch holding a tire, that fat and black rubber noose. It's perfectly still. With no breeze the hot air sits, searing human and tree skin alike, ready to boil. Somebody should have the heart to take the swing down and put it out of its misery, but no one does. Everybody around here lets things destroy themselves beyond their time, waiting for Christ's expiration date. Because when somebody or something dies or bleeds out, it's the Lord's time and there's no use in interfering with any of that.

Harper watches the house and watches Job from behind the fence for two hours. She's almost sober when he's done. Job collects his things, and swings his bag over his shoulder as he walks towards the bleachers. She lights a cigarette to dull the rattle inside her head and ease the emptiness of her mouth. One of the kids Job is with whispers into his ear then points towards her. Job turns, leaving the other kids behind. Harper's feet stutter and she's still. Wasting the cigarette, she takes one more drag before grinding it out in the dust. He's walking quickly, then he's jogging, the bag banging into his legs in heavy beats. He stalks closer and he's sprinting. Giving her a real smile, he wraps his arms around her waist and plunges his face into the nape of her neck. His face, damp with sweat and dirt, slides over her skin.

'Hi,' he says.

Harper says nothing while feeling his not so little body pressing into hers. The long, thin muscles underneath the skin of his arms lock her in. He holds her. He's holding her.

'Hi,' she says.

As he steps back, he removes his hat with its yellowing sweat ring bleaching the brim, and repositions it back onto his head, cocked slightly to the right. His dark hair is pressed in sweaty mats to his skull, wet looking and dirty. 'You're taller.'

'Not by much. But you are.' Harper takes the bag from his shoulder and slings it onto hers as they walk together.

'Stayin at home?'

'Yeah, for now.'

From the field they walk past the elementary school. Abandoned in summer, the brick building rots, its edges crumbling, waiting for a concrete implosion. They head towards the patches of dead grass lining the main road. She pulls the creased pack of cigarettes from her pocket and shakes one loose. She inhales as the tip ignites in her hands.

'Can I get one?'

'No,' she says, sliding Her lighter into her back pocket.

'Let me get one.'

'No.' Harper smiles.

'You know, you look like Her—when you do stuff that's bad for you. You look like Her.'

'That so?' Harper smiles still.

'Cmon, let me get one?'

'Nah, shit'll kill you. Poison'll kill you. Aint your time to die.'

'How bout you then? Shit'll kill you too.'

'Don't say shit, only trash swear,' she says. 'You look real good—out there I mean. You're pretty good.'

'Yeah?' He kicks a rock a yard ahead with the plastic toe of his cleat.

Cars speed by in sporadic intervals. A few times, Harper grabs him by the collar of his shirt, yanking him closer to her and away from the road.

'I got a game next week. Come if you aint dead by then.'

She tosses the butt onto the ground and extinguishes the burning filter with her shoe. The ground is nothing but layers of dead. Brown on brown. Sunlight dies when its rays sink into the earth. 'Happy?'

'Collier comes to my games,' he says, picking up a rock and tossing it high into the air. He catches it.

'Yeah?'

'Yep—thinks she's good luck.'

Harper smiles at the thought of Collier sitting in the bleachers and thinking someone needs her. Thinking she has a reason to be somewhere. Thinking she has a reason to do something.

'Yeah, maybe she is.'

'I think so, I told her I think she is but she told me I'm the only one who thinks that. You been to the house yet?'

Harper nods.

'I got bunk beds now and Aunt Denise lives with us.'

'How long she been round?'

'Since the mornin they made Mama leave.'

Harper says nothing, just watches over her shoulder as the empty old house with the sinking roof and that shed full of firsts get smaller and smaller behind them. They're a foot closer to home with each stride. The walk home is littered with road kill. They pass the rotting carcass of a doe sprawled near the intersection. It reeks of hot metal and old meat. The doe's stomach and chest cavity are torn open and its head is twisted backwards so it faces it hind legs. Job pokes the body with a stick and Harper gives him a hard smack to the back of the head. He curses, protesting he just wants to make sure it's dead.

'Aunt Denise is okay. She cooks tons and cleans and that kinda stuff.'

'She's your maid.' Harper flicks his ear. 'That's why ya like her.'

'She's helpin out is all,' he says, swatting at her hand.

'Bet she is.'

'She's nice—honest she is.'

No matter where she's walking from, it always takes the same amount of time to get home. Dilapidated buildings and storefronts masquerade as a town. The street corners are no more than piles of rubble and chunks of busted concrete with the occasional traffic light or broken stop sign. All of it built and sitting heavy on red clay, dry and real thirsty earth. Cars bounce over potholes on their rickety frames as they trail down the uneven road, bucking and dipping along. Harper and Job turn onto their street lined with would-be gardens drowning in decaying crabgrass and mounds of old mulch. Windows hang lazily on the house fronts. Summer heat melts the wood frames into splintered frowns.

'We should go see Her,' Harper says, 'Her birthday in a couple months. She'll be the same age Jesus was when He got murdered.'

'Daddy won't drive us.'

'Caro will. She said she would.'

'Oh. You gonna get Her somethin for Her birthday?'

'Dunno, maybe a grandkid.'

'Gross,' he says, 'that's gross.'

'How about you then?'

'Dunno.'

'How you do in school?'

'Okay, I guess. It's borin.'

'Caro goes to college.'

'Yeah, I know,' he says. 'Tommy played baseball in college. In Florida—Florida like with all them beaches—but he don't no more.'

'Yeah, cause he's a piece a shit.'

'Cause why?'

'Cause that's what he is cause that's what his daddy is so that's all he'll ever be.'

'I'm real glad you're home but I bet you're more glad than anybody.' He smiles to himself and pitches a rock as hard as he can down the street. It falls a few feet short of a red Toyota missing its fender and Harper says nothing.

'What's first thing you ate when you got out?' he asks.

'Grilled cheese.'

'Knew it, I shoulda bet you.'

'Should have.'

'I'm starvin,' Job says.

Eleven, Eleven and Thirteen

Job weeps.

'He sure cry an awful lot,' Caro says, pouring a handful of peanuts into her mouth.

'Harper, where's your Mama at?' Collier's hair is even lighter this summer, so blonde and sun-bleached it's almost white. You'd think she was an angel if she wasn't always flying so close to hell.

'Prolly sleepin or somethin.'

Summer's pulse is slower, faint with boredom, sunburns, and long afternoons spent at the dirty kitchen table. The day slinks by as Caro rolls her eyes at Collier who sinks low into her chair, feeling her pocket to make sure her mama's cigarettes are still there.

'You got anythin else to eat? Your Mama make dinner soon?'

'She don't fix dinner when She's tired.'

The door down the hall next to Job's nursery opens and She rises. Gently ricocheting down the hall and into the kitchen, She uses Her elbows to guide Her path. The unraveling hem of Her shorts graces the tops of Her thighs. A tattered black bra covers most of Her chest and She sighs when She sees the three of them.

'Mornin gals,' She says, pushing past Harper and Collier to the refrigerator. Raking Her fingers through Her hair, She gazes into the fridge before slamming it shut. She kisses both Caro and Collier on the tops of their heads then leans down to bring Harper's face to Hers, kissing her on the mouth. She breathes into Harper and Her thin lips taste sour but wonderful with Her eyelids fluttering and a smile curling upwards. Opening the fridge again, She pulls two bottles with the labels scratched off and a gallon of orange juice from the bottom shelf then the ice cube tray from the freezer. Job's wails hit a higher pitch. She winces, shuts Her eyes but says nothing as She mixes the three liquids into a tumbler. The colours mix into a cloudy, dead brown. Juice and liquor lap over the rim of the glass and settle in shallow pools on the countertop. She flings a handful of ice towards Her glass and two cubes fall short, landing on the floor. Collier picks them up and drops them carefully into the glass.

'How long he been cryin?' Her breaths are shallow and Her hands are anxious, twitching and hungry for touch.

'Dunno.' Collier answers before Harper has a chance to. Collier never takes her eyes off Her. She seldom even blinks in Her presence and it's the way that Collier watches Her that Harper doesn't like. Collier has her own mama to keep secrets with. Harper wishes she was strong enough to hate Collier— strong like Caro is strong but Harper isn't and never has been.

'Aint nobody talkin to you, Ann-Collier. Harper, said how long he been cryin now?'

'Dunno, M'am.'

'He shouldn't—he shouldn't cry like that. Somethin— somethin's wrong. Go to your brother.' Her face is flushed. Blood rises, pressing upwards against her flesh in crimson patches on her neck, chest and arms. 'Your brother wants you.'

Harper says nothing as She bites her bottom lip then runs Her tongue over Her bottom gums.

'He wants you.' Her gaze settles on the windowsill's long-dead geraniums. 'Your brother needs you.' She takes a long swig and kneels in front of Harper. 'You never cried, not never. Not even when you caught the counter that night.' She runs Her thumb over the faint scar on Harper's forehead. 'All your life you laughed, no cryin, never. I hate it when he cries. You girls go in there to help him back to sleep, gone there and hug him a bit, all right? Make sure he's okay.' She exhales a breath into Harper and the taste makes her hungry and happy.

'Yes, M'am.'

She kisses Harper again then rises, grabbing the glass from the counter. Pinching Collier's hip as She leaves, Collier's body coils into itself.

'He's just a baby is all,' Caro whispers. 'He don't know better.'

She kisses Caro whose mouth is a straight line and eyes are hard and jaw is clenched and she looks more like Tillie than she ever has. Strong like Tillie's strong.

'Yall be good,' She calls and the door slams behind Her.

Collier walks to the counter and drags her thumb through the puddle She's made. Collier sucks on her finger. 'She's always tired now.'

'She aint tired,' Caro says. 'Stop sayin She's tired—She aint tired.'

Harper takes a swallow before handing the bottle to Collier. Everyone allowed to be thirsty. No shame in that. Collier coughs then spits over Caro. Harper laughs, Caro rolls her eyes and wipes her arms and chest. The bourbon slides down Harper's throat and burns her insides, again.

They pass the bottle back and forth until Caro pukes in the sink. Collier hides the vomit-soaked dishes with three paper towels and dumps her mama's cigarettes on top. Job's hysterical sobs still ring through Harper's daddy's house.

'Christ, yall not understand?' Her voice slinks through the plaster and into their ears while Her clamped fist punches the wall.

'Maybe he's—he's, uh, he's hungry.' Harper's body pinballs, retracing Her steps. Her flesh is pink, blushing from her cheeks to her chest and her hands are dead at her hips.

He stands in his crib, a scrawny prisoner, his boy body convulsing as he sobs. Damp stains and spit up are drying on his t-shirt. His face and hands are smeared with tears and puke. Beating his balled up fists against the side of the crib, he's shaking as hard as he can. He's thrown his blanket and stuffed sheep onto the floor. Caro picks them up and softly sets them back into his crib then places her own hand on Job's small fist and whispers something to him Harper can't make out.

'We have to make him stop.'

'She could if She wanted,' Harper says. 'She'd make him stop.'

'Yall say stupid shit sometimes—he's hungry is all.' Caro's

hands trace the crib's railing while Harper struggles to untangle his limbs from the spokes of the crib.

'What'd you know bout feedin babies?' Collier sneers.

'Know more than you, asshole.'

Harper's head barely makes it to the top of the crib, but Collier clears her by a full head and easily pulls Job out by his arms. She turns to hand him to Harper just as his body thrashes with a howl, and she loses hold of him. He meets the floor with a sharp thud and he's silent, his eyes unblinking, wide and alert. Collier's paralyzed limbs hang at her sides.

'It's fine, She do it all the time. It's fine—I swear.' Harper picks Job off the floor then holds him to her chest, like she's seen Her do a few times. When She holds Job real tight and he falls asleep so quick with his head resting against Her chest, Her heartbeat pulsing against his soft ear, keeping time for him and his little boy body. Those couple of times She finally convinced him to get some sleep. With his eyes shut, mouth open, fingers twitching, his shallow breaths claimed Her body and he was a beautiful little boy. He can be so pretty that sometimes Harper wonders why God didn't make him a little girl. Looking so beautiful when he sleeps, and when he sleeps he's safe.

Job's snot, tears and puke paint Harper's neck slick. He buries his face into her chest and she presses him into her, trying to quiet him, make him feel her quickening pulse. Harper cradles him the best she can and his cries die, but his silent sobs shake both of their bodies.

'Please, please, please, Harper—don't tell Her I drop him,' Collier says under her breath. 'Didn't mean to, honest I didn't.'

'Here,' Caro says, holding a rotting banana with skin covered in black patches. Caro peels it and smears a bit onto her fingers. 'All I could find—it's fine though cause it's soft so he can eat it.' She gently pushes them into his mouth as the gaze of his dark eyes bounce from the banana to the shame on Collier's unwashed face. He sucks on Caro's fingers and she smiles. 'See, he just hungry is all. Told you so, asshole.'

She got real sad after you was born. Not because She didn't love you, but because She was tired and Her insides ached and people thought She was sick but She wasn't. And because Her body turned against Her.

She spent all day and all night alone in Her room. I never saw Her anymore and I hated you sometimes because when She tried to feed you, you'd push Her away, beat your little balled up fists against Her. You didn't want Her. You didn't want Her body anymore because you were done with Her. But I don't blame you for nothing. If you had been a little girl and known that your body was Hers and Hers was yours, like me, things probably would have been different. You probably wouldn't have cried as much neither.

I think about you crying a lot. 'Don't cry because things aint that bad—things could be worse,' Caro had told me once. But it was a real long time after Collier dropped you that Caro told me not to cry.

Nineteen, Nineteen and Twenty-One

Job runs from the street towards the house, waving at Collier who sits on the hood of Tommy's parked truck, hugging her knees while she smokes.

'Where you been?' she says, grinding the cigarette against the windshield.

'Nowhere.'

'Liar. Caro said you didn't come by last night.'

'Don't ask questions you already know answers to then.'

'Where you been?'

'I didn't get a chance to see Caro.'

'That so? You been wearing the same clothes three days now.' Collier pulls at the bottom of Harper's shirt.

'I look like shit—'

'What you look like is trash. You never look like this after Charlie—you hear from him?'

'Have you?' Harper says.

'No. Just up and left, right after you did. Heard he found him some rich girl up in D.C. or Baltimore. He's garbage.'

'He say bye?'

'Said bye to Tommy but not me or Caro.'

Harper says nothing.

'But Mike—Mike's a real piece of trash. Don't make that no habit. You get sick and swell actin stupid like that.'

Harper leans into the truck, pressing her back against the passenger's side door. It burns through her shirt but she's too exhausted to move. 'I won't.'

'You seen your daddy yet?' Collier asks.

'Yeah.'

'He home now?'

'Dunno.'

'You all right?'

'Sure,' Harper says.

'Sure?'

'Yeah.'

'All right then, if you so sure, cmon.'

'Should prolly change.'

'Don't need to change for this.'

'What?' Harper climbs into the truck, watching Collier squinting in the sun with a lazy grin hanging from her empty mouth.

'Nothin.'

'What?'

Collier lets her thumb trace the white line running from Harper's middle finger to her wrist. 'I think about that knife we cut ourselves with every day.'

Ten, Ten and Twelve

It's not sinful, this time. Not sinful like the last time they tried. This time it's considered and slow and they use the pocketknife with a red handle Collier lifted from Tommy's tackle box.

'Where we suppose to cut?' Caro asks.

'Finger,' Collier says, while they walk deeper into the woods shoulder to shoulder to the chorus of purring crickets and gunshot echoes.

'I guess just nick it a good bit.' Caro grabs the knife from Collier then snaps the small blade open. 'Yeah, so take it like this—' Touching the point of the blade to her fingertip, she traces an invisible line down to the base of her palm.

'You gone slit your wrist, give it here.' Collier snatches the knife back and quickly pushes the dulled tip into her finger, twisting the blade, digging carefully into her skin. Red rises to the surface. 'Here, gone then.'

Caro clenches her teeth and scowls as she presses the knife into her flesh then drags it from her middle fingertip down. A dark line seeps slowly from where the blade had been.

'You all right?'

'Yep,' Caro says, watching her blood trickle down her hand.

When it's Harper's turn, she makes a small incision in her middle finger. Nothing leaks so she cuts deeper to draw blood like Caro and Collier but losing grip on the handle, slices a deep cut from her middle finger down to her wrist.

'Stop, that's too much.' Caro can't take her real wide eyes off the bleeding track. 'Make it stop—'

Before Collier inhales her next breath, she pulls at her shirttail and holds it tight against Harper's pulse. Her blood runs thick and black spitting from her wrist and Caro's face is white.

'It's fine, don't look at it Caro, Jesus.' Collier's grip tightens on Harper's arm. 'Witches do it all the time. Don't worry, I'll make sure you all right.'

'I know,' Harper says. The skin over Collier's knuckles is pulled tight as she holds onto Harper's wrist still. They watch each other for a real long time. Caro's lips twitch like she's saying something, but no sounds come out. Collier presses her own bleeding finger to Caro's before dragging it through the stream running down Harper's forearm. Caro softly touches

Harper's blood and then grasps Collier's hand. Their blood runs together, red smearing over their hands and wrists until they can't tell whose is whose.

'Shouldn't we say somethin?' Caro says. 'Maybe I should pray or somethin?'

Holding Harper's pulse with her bare hand, Collier lets them be silent—it's the only time she doesn't yell, or cackle, or fill the empty air. 'I'll kill myself if yall ever leave,' Collier finally says and releases Harper when she knows good and well the bleeding has stopped. Collier's hands are soaked in their blood. She wipes the blade clean against her bare leg, snaps the knife shut and slides it into her back pocket.

Collier held me to make sure nothing bad happened. She kept a steady hand and she's the only person I ever known who knew how to use her hands. Not just build something someone else told her, but really make something. Sometimes though, seemed to me the only reason she made things was so she could tear them down. But she loved doing things knowing everything would turn out fine, unless she decided they wouldn't. It wasn't that she was addicted to anything, it was just that she liked knowing that when she did something it would leave her feeling good. And everything else was just another disappointment.

Nineteen, Nineteen and Twenty-One

Leaves hang lifeless on brittle branches. Tree bark peels off itself, crumbles and collects in piles on the ground. Slack tree roots line the floor of the woods. A cardinal with a deep red chest puffed out underneath its black beard and greasy crimson feathers lands on a broken root. Its beak is pinched shut.

'Against law to kill a cardinal,' Harper says. 'You can other places, but not here.'

The truck is left running, its exhaust pipe breathing thick smut into the air.

'No shit?'

They sit in the back of the truck, swapping sips and lazy smiles to *Paul's Boutique*. The bass throbs against old speakers in a dull buzz, and the rusted tailgate rubs the backs of their thighs raw.

'—tastes terrible,' Harper says, taking a pull from the glass bottle. 'Tastes cheap.'

'Tommy left it out.'

'Where he been?'

'In and out.'

'Where's Gina?'

'Florida.'

'She was a real treat.'

Collier laughs. 'Her folks real rich.'

'Where's Caro at?'

Collier fills her mouth, sloshing whiskey from cheek to cheek like mouthwash before swallowing. 'Class or work prolly. She always somewhere else now—she always got somethin now.'

Harper sets the bottle between her legs as Collier rummages through her bag. She palms an orange pill bottle that Harper grabs from her. Collier snatches it back.

'Careful now.' The top pops off and Collier pours four orange capsules into her hand. Her hair hangs in front of her face and Harper can't see her eyes, only that smile spreading something thick.

'What's at?'

'It matter?' Collier says, placing two on her tongue. Harper does the same. 'It's just medicine.'

'Oh.' Harper picks at her cuticles because she aches every time she looks at them. Scratching at her nail beds because she doesn't have a scab. Seeing Tara Hackett every time she catches a glimpse of her own hands.

They tread in silence, passing the bottle, covering it with their grease and saliva and sweat and smiles. The bottle's mouth is pink from their lips. Their eyelids droop heavier in their steady rhythm of swigs. They giggle at nothing, waiting for the other to say something—to kill the silence, to fill the void like they used to. Collier's scared of silence so she takes longer and longer pulls from the bottle when it's her turn, Harper pushes down each mouthful, feels sunlight bleed onto her flesh.

'How's your Mama?'

'Don't,' Harper says.

'Why?'

'Jesus—cmon.'

Collier stills and her lips are hushed. Her tongue hides behind her teeth and she bites her bottom lip until it turns purple. 'I'm sorry, Harper.'

'What you sorry for then?'

'I dunno, but I am—'

'You sound like an idiot when you say shit like that.'

'I prayed you'd still look like Her.'

'Shut up, Collier.'

'—even though you meaner than She is—'

'—stop sayin stupid shit—'

'—more tired than She ever was—'

'She aint dead.'

'Not yet,' Collier says. 'Neither are you. What am I suppose to do when you are?'

'Burn me. I aint sleepin in the ground. Then you snort the ashes if you want.'

Collier tips her head back, laughing long, smiling with her whole body as it eases. The tension leaving her limbs as she cackles and Harper smiles too.

'I'm the best high you'll ever have,' Harper says.

'Don't I know it.' Collier scoffs and smiles still. 'If you could, could snort anyone's ashes—who'd it be? And you can't pick Jesus.'

'Why?'

'Cause he didn't have no ashes. Sides, who wants snort Christ?'

'Dunno, aint never thought about anythin like at. It's like, straight ashes, or is there other shit in it?' Harper's mouth receives the bottle.

'Just ashes.'

'Couldn't just snort straight ashes.'

'Since when you so picky? Good Lord, it's just a game.'

'Caro'd hate this game. I dunno—bout you then?'

'Well, I'd have Lucille Ball,' Collier says.

'So what about a man?' Harper's hand slips along the neck of the bottle, nearly dropping it.

'Careful, don't waste none.'

'What—bout a man?'

'Prolly John Wayne. Cowboys are faggots.'

'I'd have, I dunno—' Harper sighs, 'maybe Vivien Leigh.'

'I'd have Scarlett O'Hara,' Collier says and smiles real big so Harper has to smile too.

'Course you would.'

Collier keeps smiling and bounces from side to side, trying to find the perfect cadence in her drunk. The one to make her feel safe and brave and strong. Harper watches her and sees what she's always seen but Collier won't hold her gaze for more than a second. They pass the bottle back and forth until their heads bloat and their mouths swell with laughter again and they're sweaty.

'Bet we could make millions off famous people ashes.'

'Sure we could,' Harper says. 'You the only rich girl I'd ever have.'

'You uh, you got like, like any money or anythin?' Collier's still smiling and swaying, like she's listening to a song Harper can't hear.

'Nope.' Harper's head bounces forward and back, nodding for no reason, answering a question that hasn't been asked.

'Your daddy give ya money?'

'Since when he ever give me anythin?'

'I need money.'

'You ask Caro?'

'She think she better than me now. Think she better than us. Coward is what she is.'

'Don't talk like that.'

Collier glares at her and takes another small dark bottle from her purse. She unscrews the top and drinks until she's done. Harper watches her eyes get real big and bright like a slot machine, reeling and reeling. But now things are blurring together in Harper's eyes and mind and things would be better if it wasn't so hot all the time.

'You forgive her too much. If she done to me what she done to you—I'd gut her the minute I got out,' Collier says, 'Caro forgot who she is, but I aint. I never would have left you like she did—'

'Christ, you don't know shit about shit sometimes. I swear, Collier.' Harper's words are barely a whisper, they're just the hot breaths her Mama taught her. 'I wanna crack your skull when you talk like that. And guess what else—she didn't leave me, I left her—'

Collier is silent. Her mouth is empty as her glance falls from Harper to the ground and she shrugs. There's a tremor in her hands. She hasn't looked this way in a long time. But Caro isn't here to defend herself and Harper is too tired to do it anymore.

'What'd you need?' Harper doesn't know what's in the bottle but it tastes like piss and aluminum and then nothing at all. Swallowing three mouthfuls she offers it back to Collier.

'Finish it,' she says.

Harper turns the bottle upside down and empties it.

'I'm real late,' Collier says, her eyes unmoving and fixed on a pile of dry bark.

Harper tosses the empty bottle onto the ground as her stomach lurches into her throat. She tastes a spew of bile and swallows it back down. 'How much?'

'Month and a half or so.'

'You don't look it.'

'Lucky girl, huh?'

'You won't take—'

'You sure bout that?' Collier asks.

'What bout Tommy?'

'He done the last couple. Told me to drink it way. But there's no tellin with at. Might just come out retard.'

Harper holds Collier's hand, not because she wants to, but because it's the easiest thing to do. 'I'm sorry.' Their palms press together and Harper feels her pulse matched in Collier's.

'Nothin to be sorry for.' Collier hops from the tailgate and steadies herself in the dry earth. With her chest and cheeks flushed pink, she bends over and grabs the larger glass bottle from the ground. She gives it to Harper then places a hand on each hip, standing with her feet a shoulder width apart. A slaughtered Wonder Woman. 'Well, cmon then—'

Harper closes her eyes and shakes her head, feeling her eyeballs bounce from one side of her skull to the other.

'Don't be like that, just a couple now—just a couple swings. Real quick.' Collier smiles, shaking a cigarette loose from the pack in her back pocket then lights it. She exhales a wisp of blue smoke in Harper's direction. 'That's not what I said when you needed it—I said yes for Caro when she need it. Never said no to either of you. Never. When I ever said no to you?'

'I aint thirteen no more.' Harper jumps from the truck bed and flips the bottle so she's gripping its neck and her hand doesn't feel like her own.

'You owe me.' Collier grins. 'You owe me. Whatcha, whatcha, whatcha want? You afraid you remember how much you like it? Cmon, just pretend I'm your Mama.'

Harper draws the bottle back and swings it forward. It meets Collier's mouth. 'Sorry.' Harper laughs and stretches for Collier's hand but she loses her balance and falls onto the ground herself.

'Aint no baby in my throat,' Collier cackles, sucking in real sharp breaths. They laugh and laugh and laugh. She bites her forearm to make sure all of her teeth are still there then drags her fingertips through the blood trickling from her lips to her chin and spits. She stops wheezing and rises to her feet.

'Strike one then. Cmon now, someone's gettin evicted.' Collier giggles with her dry lips split open and Harper can't help but do the same. Collier's smile and teeth are painted in a smear of blood from her leaking top gums. Harper keeps smiling while she strikes her in the stomach. Collier doubles over and her knees meet the ground. She's kneeling again—kneeling like she's praying before Harper. Praying for mercy. That's what Harper would have prayed for if she was Collier. Would have prayed for mercy from Christ himself—if Harper was her, but she isn't.

Collier wheezes and cackles still. Her howls bounce through trees and she gasps for full breaths, holding her stomach. Eyes shut, she rolls from side to side like some frail beetle caught on its backside. Harper takes a long drag from the cigarette and peers into the bottle, still thirsty. There's no shame in it. You allowed to be thirsty. And Collier allowed to be thirsty too. But the bottle is empty, like it was before. Like it always is because it's always empty. Then Harper hits Collier again because she loves Collier and Collier is her sister. Harper avoids her face but sees Collier's jaw is a bit bruised and Harper's sure that bruise—that bruise, that bruise there is old and tired. And it's just a bruise, nothing serious, it won't even scar. Just a purple kiss with funny edges is all. Tommy's fading good night kiss is all. Collier catches her breath and Harper reaches for her, pulling her to her feet.

'You all right?'

'I—worried—afraid you uh, couldn't, couldn't take care yourself.'

'What?'

'When you gone—I was scared ya couldn't take care of yourself. But now—you took uh, took care of yourself. I know it. Even though ya won't say nothin, I know it. Caro gets scared when you quiet. She hate it when you quiet but I know. You don't got to say it.' Collier's hunched over with her hands on her knees, breathless and raining blood from her mouth. 'You didn't need no dyke take care of you, huh?'

Harper's hand isn't her own because the bottle's not no bottle at all her eyes close maybe they aren't closed hitting Collier in the stomach cause she asked me to because she done it for me twice once for Caro I hit Charlie in the face because he left without a word found a nice girl with nice words and doesn't puke in bed I hit Tara Hackett in the stomach cause maybe it would hurt there least doctors said Tara Hackett's infected but it wasn't her fault she done what she done don't everybody need to be a mama when I crack Caro's skull in two a piece for me a piece for Collier Caro Tillie's girl think she better than us forgetting everything happen to us when it was his turn I hit my daddy for thinking me and Job aint his I hit Her in the belly full of soak and swallows and pills cause She don't make me dinner no more want to know my secrets no more She aint here no more I can't look after Her if She aint here don't She know that I kicked Collier between the legs because babies can be real stubborn I heard that one time punched Collier because I am saving the little girl inside her hitting our little girl more to make sure she won't never grow to know pain like we did I lost count how many daughters Collier drank away how many daughters felt the raw ridges of Tommy's clamped fist will this little girl the one I am saving will you know me if you ever come out if I ever let you breathe but you can't hate me the way Collier hates you do you know that you could have been mine Tommy been in me before more than once will you know many girls meCaroCollierI saved?

Collier's saying something. It could be 'stop' or 'harder' or 'yes, M'am,' or 'another' or 'please' or 'I love you.' Something's said but it doesn't matter because there's not much difference between all the words it could have been. And Harper stops.

Sweat runs from her temples to her ears and it feels like she's swimming in the deep end, when you hold your breath and sink lifeless to the bottom, sitting with your eyes closed and hearing only echoes. The pressure winding tighter and tighter inside your ears until all the oxygen is gone and you have no choice but to float, defeated. God pulls you to the surface, making you drink air again because He won't let you die. You haven't earned that yet so you're forced to breathe.

Harper pockets the glass bottle's cap and she wants to puke but nothing comes up. Dry heaving, she waits for her mind to slow, praying for it to stutter. Collier lies on the ground with her eyes bulging from their sockets. Her shallow panting is the only thing Harper hears. She places her hand on Collier's face before helping her stand. And Collier rises, grasping at Harper's shoulders and hips, grasping at her angles. She wipes blood from her face with the back of her hand and leans down, pressing her face into Harper's neck. Collier's blonde, blood-streaked hair is matted across her face.

'Jesus,' Collier breathes, taking the cigarette from Harper's mouth and placing it into her own. She takes a drag then returns the tightly-rolled and blood-spattered body to Harper's lips. Collier's blood tastes an awful lot like Harper's, like Tara Hackett's, like Sister Josephine Paul's. She gives Harper's empty hand a squeeze then kisses Harper's cheek. Collier's tongue traces the trail of blood left along Harper's jaw. This time, Harper lets her.

'Sorry,' Harper whispers.

'You mean that?'

Harper looks at the ground and shakes her head. 'No.'

'Don't be sad—you earned it, huh? You did good,' Collier says, 'think we got her.'

'This is the worst thing I ever done?'

Collier cackles with her teeth still straight and blood soaked, bruises already pushing through her flesh. 'Not even close.'

I never seen a cardinal since that day. Not one. But I still got that whiskey cap hidden underneath the nightstand next to my bed. Keep it tucked away because don't want them thinking I been sneaking out or drinking or getting messed up or anything like that. If they thought I was doing stuff like that, they'd kick me out. Then I'd have to find somewhere else handing out free meals and hot water and forgiveness. I'd have to flee to a new place that saves the filthy fallen.

Sometimes after curfew I can't fall asleep because of their voices. So sometimes after curfew the only thing I hear is Jenny's coming and going and breathing and crying. Sometimes after curfew I take out that whiskey cap and run my fingertip along the small ridges of its edge. Sometimes, if their voices are too loud, I put the cap in my mouth and let my tongue taste it. It's dry, like red earth, like summer. And it tastes like how Collier used to taste and Collier used to taste how I think hate tastes. Metal. Dust. And heat.

Collier had enough hate for everyone—didn't matter what colour they was or who they prayed to, didn't matter what was between their legs. She hated everyone who looked at her wrong. Hated everyone who called her trash. But Collier wasn't real trash. Collier was numbers. With a fifth and a half of ditch whiskey and a pack of cigarettes, it took Collier no time at all to give me back what I thought I lost and she showed me that nothing had changed. Collier showed me my sin. Things hadn't changed because Collier wouldn't let them. Collier liked things the way she thought they should be. That's why Collier was numbers and patterns and why she let things, the same stupid things, keep happening over and over and over again. Collier did who and what pleased her over and over again until she didn't.

I talk about Collier because she's never quiet. And I figure maybe, if I talk for her now, things will be quiet for me. Collier wasn't reckless like most everyone thought, she was real considered and she was beautiful too.

Nineteen, Nineteen and Twenty-One

'What happened?' Caro says.

Collier's eye sockets are hollow and blackened. Dark bags hang heavy under her muted, blue-grey eyes.

'Nothin,' Harper says.

'What happened?'

Collier looks at Harper and away from Caro, waiting for someone to tell her what to do. Waiting for someone to fill the silence.

'Yall in trouble?' Caro asks.

'Jesus, Caro, shut up,' Collier says.

'What do yall want me to say? You don't tell me anything—'

'We don't tell you nothin, Carolyn?' Collier pauses and squeezes Harper's hand underneath the table. 'You aint even around no more and I'm broke and what else—'

'You still fifteen? How old are you? Same stupid stuff with you—always—'

'Don't be act like it's different because it aint. Don't act like you different than me. You done a same thing too. You both done it plenty.'

Caro rolls her eyes and digs her bright pink fingernails into the Styrofoam cup, leaving deep lines where she's been. 'Tommy's a piece of shit and you're stupid as hell for thinking—'

'We got it,' Harper says.

'You did this?'

'Yeah.'

'So, yall going to like, order somethin or just sit all day just takin up space?' Mike calls from the back.

'Shut up, aint nobody talkin to you, moron,' Collier yells.

70

Caro's face isn't surprised or disgusted or sympathetic or relieved. It's nothing. Caro is blank. Caro is nothing.

'You wanna say somethin?' Harper says, looking into her, thinking that maybe Collier had been right—that Caro thinks she's different from them now. So high and mighty.

'It take?' Caro surrenders.

Opening the pack in her bag, Harper hands a cigarette to Collier. 'We'll find out,' she says, placing it on the table and pushing it over to Caro. 'Here.'

'I quit.' Caro's cigarette sits untouched.

'Since when?'

'Tillie didn't raise no quitter.'

'They'll kill you, you know,' she says, leaning back into the booth.

'Nah, they won't. One time I read if you quit before you're twenty-five you'll never get addicted to nothin.'

'Collier, that has got to be the dumbest damn thing I ever heard. And since when—since when do you read shit?'

The bell on the door rattles when he forces it open. They're silent when Tommy enters, like always. A bad habit to be broken that never will be. Collier and Harper return their cigarettes to the table as he stalks over. His jeans hang over his heels and drag along the ground, unraveling hems scraping the filthy floor and collecting grease. He smiles at Harper, seeing only her. No matter where they are or who they're with, his mass takes up the bulk of a room. He is tall, lean. His body is as sturdy as it's always been. Arms like tree trunks, smooth and unscarred. The long muscles have always been there, even when they were little. But somehow, he's still a boy with his messy mop of hair, sawdust coloured and shoved underneath a baseball cap. The tops of his ears are sunkissed pink from working and drinking in the sun. It's hard to see the other parts of his face when he smiles. His face is all smile. He's still a boy. He's a boy until death. But he's always strong meat.

Wrapping his arms around her, Tommy picks Harper up from her seat with ease. Sweat, tobacco, the sour stink of chemicals fills her lungs. The scruff of his face rubs her cheek raw. Pressing the planks of his chest into her tits, she feels weak, soft in her own skin. He's hard. Holding her hips in place, he presses himself into her. He holds her so tight she can barely breathe. He holds her until he's done with her.

'You aint change none,' he says, with a rough hand on each side of her face. 'Not a bit. It's like your mama here.' Sometimes he lets himself be pretty. Sometimes, he lets himself be beautiful. He kisses her, flicking his tongue into her mouth, branding her in a touch she can't shake.

'You neither.'

Caro won't look him in the eye and her lips twitch but no words or sounds come out. Collier casts her gaze out the window.

'Now you,' he says to Collier, taking Harper's seat next to her, 'you look like trash.' He kisses the fresh bruise on her neck and she flinches as his lips meet her skin. 'Good night, huh?' He winks at Caro and pulls at one of Collier's sleeves exposing a wet, black-edged cut. She yanks down her shirt, scooting closer to the window.

'It's always a good night,' Collier says.

'How about you, Caro? You too? You learn to hold your liquor yet?'

Caro says nothing as she grabs the cigarette and Luce's lighter from the table. The bell rings her exit as she pushes through the doors. In the parking lot, she lights the cigarette and smokes alone.

'What's wrong with her?' He finishes her cup, chomping the ice with his molars.

'She tired is all,' Harper says. 'School and workin lots.'

'I know—we all know.' Tommy drapes his arm across Collier's shoulders, pulling her in close. 'How long you been out?'

'Few days.'

'How's it then?'

'How's what?'

'In there—what's it like in there?'

'Lay off her.' Collier watches Caro pace.

'Aint nobody talkin to you, Ann-Collier. Harper, I said what's it like in there?'

'Don't,' Collier whispers into the window still watching Caro taking long drags with her head bowed, taking her time.

'Okay, I guess.'

He bursts into laughter and Collier tries to hide a smile but can't. She loves it when he laughs. She always has.

'Okay?' he says. 'You guess it was okay?'

'Yeah—it's okay.'

'Got yourself a girlfriend? You somebody's wife?'

'Were you?' Collier asks.

Fifteen, Fifteen and Seventeen

'Harper?'

And Harper says nothing.

'I hear you—I said get down here.'

And Harper says nothing.

'Don't make me ask you again.'

Harper's bare feet sting as they plant on the concrete floor.

'Lay down.' Tara Hackett's body is wrapped in a cotton blanket, separating their skins. 'You cold, sweetheart?'

'No.' Harper is a straight line, head to toe, stiff and waiting.

Tara Hackett runs her fingertips inside the waistband of Harper's pants, tracing the faint veins at the crook of her hip. 'Cold as a corpse. Don't lie to me again. Lyin a sin. Aint your Mama ever taught you that?'

And Harper says nothing.

'Say yes—say yes, m'am.'

'Yes, m'am.'

'Say you sorry for lyin.'

'I'm sorry for lyin.'

'Mean it?'

'Yes, m'am.'

'Good. You ought not lie to me again.'

'I won't lie to you again.'

'Now, tell me bout your Mama.'

Harper stares at the furthest corner of the cell between the toilet and the sink. At night, in the dark, their flesh is invisible and Harper sees nothing. Everything is blacker than the backs of her eyelids and it's hours and hours until breakfast.

'I said tell me bout your Mama. Tell me ya look like Her.'

'I look like Her.'

'What's her name?'

And Harper says nothing.

'What's her name, I said?'

'Lucille.'

'But what everyone call Her?'

'Luce.'

'What?'

'They all call Her Luce cause that's what She wanna be called.'

'Tell me you look like Her.'

'We got the same hair and the same eyes and the same smile and Collier say we smoke a cigarette the same.'

'Got same lookin bodies?'

'Yeah, I guess. She's taller. Her body has lots more angles than mine do.'

'Bet She's awful beautiful.'

'She is. I'm real lucky.'

'What do folks say when the two of you together?'

'Strangers think we're sisters.'

'Why?'

'She pretty young I guess. She only had four periods before She had me'.

74

What wouldn't stop does. Harper tastes the heat and stink of her body as Tara Hackett wraps her fingers around Harper's throat, pulling her in close and pressing her lips to Harper's ear.

'Love you, sweetheart. Just like your Mama does. That's why I take care of you while She's away.'

Harper says nothing as she climbs into her bunk, her face only a few feet beneath the ceiling. And in silence, without praying, she falls asleep. Untouched.

Nineteen, Nineteen and Twenty-One

'You hear me, Harper?' Tommy shoves a cigarette behind his ear then snaps his fingers in front of her nose.

'No.' Harper can't tell if Collier's relieved or jealous or sad. 'Nothin like that.'

'Thought it be bunch a dykes in there.'

Caro's still pacing in the parking lot with her eyes lowered to the pavement. Sunglasses with red frames cover most of her face. The cigarette is gone and her hands are jammed into her pockets.

'I dunno.'

'You lucky you didn't go to a real prison, a man's prison a real prison and a man's prison nothin but faggots who got caught. You a real lucky girl. Real lucky, gettin off so easy like you did.' He scoffs. '—bullshit dyke prison.'

And Harper says nothing.

One time She said God made Caro and Collier for me. And that the only reason we were born was to find each other. I asked Her why God gave us Tommy and She said God didn't have nothing to do with him. The Devil made Tommy and if I didn't know that already my soul was in trouble. I cried and puked that night because all I could think about was hell, and how I'd already been there. Hell was Tommy's hands and his

75

voice and his brick body and a broken ceiling fan above the locked door and Collier's silence and how I ached for days after and couldn't look nobody in the eye.

I asked Her how to get my soul out of trouble and She said She didn't know. She said if I was serious about sorting myself out I should ask Tillie about all that. 'Tillie's my favourite,' She used to say. 'Tillie's my favourite everything.'

Nineteen, Nineteen and Twenty-One

Harper rings the doorbell for the first time in her life and the blue door swings opens.

Tillie exhales, smiling real wide just like Caro does when she's happy and not faking it. 'Whatcha ring the bell for?'

Tillie's body is brittle shell of itself. Her skin is the colour of bone and her flesh grabs at her skeleton. Her collarbone juts out from her chest and Harper peeks at the scars marking where old poison pulsed. What's left of her slack tits hangs heavy as dead fish. Tillie brushes her thumbs along Harper's cheekbones, palming her face gently. Harper smells stale cigarettes and ditch weed on her fingertips.

'I prayed for you every day.' Tillie pulls Harper into her. Harper is twice the size as Tillie but not half as strong. 'Look at you, girl.' She interlocks her slender fingers with Harper's and leads her into the house.

Harper sets her shoes next to the front door before sitting on the couch. She presses her palms together and places them in her lap, crosses her legs at her ankles and happily drowns in the soft scent and colours of the room. The oak coffee table is still betrayed by Caro's initials cut deep into one of the legs, a carving that led to Caro's longest beating; a thin switch broken from the arm of a pine tree, and whipped across the back of her legs for six minutes.

'Hurts me more than it hurts you, baby girl.' Tillie smoked a cigarette and drank a Coke while thrashing her daughter's bare legs over and over and over again. Pinesap mixed with tracks of blood that ran down the backs of her skinny legs and she howled as Collier and Harper sat in silence.

'I didn't mean to cut it that much, honest,' Harper had mumbled with her head bowed, hiding Tommy's red handle pocket knife in her palm.

'You a sneaky bitch. Don't nobody know it but me,' Collier had said, sucking on a Marlboro Light pinched from Tillie's stash. 'Should be you out back, not Caro.'

'You can relax, it aint cotillion.' Tillie places her hand on the back of Harper's neck. 'Want somethin to eat? Who knows what garbage Denise fixes over at yours now? And who she tryin to prove herself to anyways? Layin with your daddy like she does—tryin to claim Job like her own cause she arid as the ground. Her and your daddy both got shit for brains.' Tillie drags her slippered feet along the uneven floorboards into the kitchen. 'Caro said she seen you. I been hopin you come round but didn't want bother ya since just you out. Just sayin this mornin I wanted you to come round and look, here you are, Harper Lucille—' She returns with a wooden tray holding a cold pulled pork sandwich with a heap of coleslaw and a bottle of Coke.

'Thanks.'

Tillie sets the tray on Harper's lap and leaning into her, kisses her forehead. Tillie's hand lingers at Harper's and their knuckles touch. 'Eat up now,' she says, pulling the rocking chair next to the table. Tillie lights a cigarette as Harper begins to eat.

'Caro studyin or somethin. Awful quiet back there. Yall three always made me nervous when yall got quiet. Quiet meant trouble. I miss that cacklin and carryin on.'

Harper smiles between large bites.

'I try not botherin her but she needs a break now and then.'

'She do good in school?'

'Yeah, real good. She works real hard now.' Tillie taps her

cigarette into the plastic ashtray resting on a King James Bible with a broken spine, big gold letters on the cover and pages as thin as her skin. 'But you always so much smarter than her.'

Twelve, Twelve and Fourteen

'—that's only cause Caro pukes like she prays—on her knees with her eyes closed asking God for another favour,' Collier mumbles through a mouthful of cherry pits.

'You shut up, my mama don't like that kinda talk.'

'Carolyn Naylor, better get in line cause everybody gone nail her.'

'Stop, give it here.' Harper grabs the plastic folder with CN etched on its cover then pulls a pencil from her backpack.

Collier stands above Harper, letting the wrinkled loose-leaf fall to the floor. 'Fix it,' she says, her lips sticky with cherry flesh, her hands slick with sweat.

'Fix it yourself. You didn't even start it—you didn't even try.'

'Hey, mine first—you aint even in our grade,' Caro says, flicking Collier's elbow.

'Shut up, moron—'

'Yall can both shut up cause yall both first.' Harper smoothes each crumpled sheet of paper flat against Tillie's Bible.

Caro rolls her eyes and falls into an armchair while Collier spins a quarter dizzily on the kitchen table, pressing her thumb onto its edge, stilling it beneath her touch.

'I can't even read this—you write like trash.' Caro's homework is a dirty sheet of half-assed guesses and lies. Its margins are decorated with five-pointed stars. CARO NAYLOR is scribbled illegibly at the top.

'It's summer soon, who cares? Just add some bits and it's done.'

Harper rubs the pink eraser against the page until there isn't a single trace of Caro. Flakes of rubber collect in piles and Harper blows at the page, clearing it. She pauses before printing *CARO NAYLOR* at the top of the page in her neatest script. For Caro, Harper is her best, her most considered. Reading each word twice, her gaze tracing the backs of consonants and the curves of vowels, Harper counts a full two Mississippis before moving forward. She rolls the pencil in her hand then writes. Each mark a straight line, clean and clear. For Caro, she's careful.

Harper watches Caro and Collier in their silence. Their lips are still and their bodies relaxed. Caro sits on the floor between Collier's outstretched legs, with her spine giving into a lazy slouch. She tugs the rubber band from her hair as Collier begins raking her fingers through Caro's dark waves, gently freeing the knots and tangles.

'Give em here.' Collier thrusts her palm open at Caro's side. Caro pulls four bobby pins from her pocket and places them in her hand. Collier pinches them between her teeth and takes a small section of Caro's hair, twirling it gently around her index and middle finger before wrapping and pinning it to Caro's skull. 'Wish my hair was dark.'

'We can dye it.'

'I wish it was suppose to be dark.'

'Collier, you spend too much time wishin for stuff that aint.'

Collier yanks at a chuck of Caro's hair, pulling her back. Her chin tilts up and a yelp escapes from her lips.

'Cut it out.' Caro elbows Collier in the ribs. 'And finish my hair.'

Caro's sheet is near perfect. The words are true and clean and right and complete. Skimming the paper branded *COLLIER Ward*, Harper pauses as her mind slows, stumbling in the doodled hearts and long-dried ink initials scratched on the page, CW & TB. The same initials Collier had carved into her forearm two weeks earlier. The four consonants that scabbed over Collier's flesh and were picked open only to heal while she flirted with the scars to come. Harper grinds the pencil tip into Tommy's initials until the ink is buried and the pointed lead breaks.

'Whatcha doin?' Collier asks, still pinning locks of Caro's hair.

'Doin your work is what I'm doin.' Harper grabs another pencil from the coffee table then stares into Collier's sheet again. She abandons punctuation, litters the paper with misspellings, run-on sentences and ill-thought fragments, filling the page with carelessness, line after line after line.

'You done yet or what?'

'Here. Yall can look now.'

'I trust you,' Collier says, folding her paper long ways twice and shoving it into a novel she'll never read.

'Yeah, thanks.' Caro slaps the paper onto the table.

'Caro, split a Coke with me.'

'Sure—my mama say only trash drink Pepsi.'

'Caro, cut that shit out, that talk aint polite.' Tillie strides through the doorway, flicking at her cigarette as ashes scatter to the floor. A pink scarf is knotted twice at her hairline and her collarbone pokes out from beneath her sleeveless blouse. Her face shines with late afternoon heat and her legs are as skinny as Caro's.

'Whatcha lookin at, girl?' Tillie says and kisses Harper's forehead. 'Bottles on the deck, Collier.'

Pushing past Caro, Collier barrels through the back door ripping the already torn screen further and Caro follows.

Tillie fingers the edge of Caro's paper, scanning the freshly written words before she rips the page four times and tosses the shreds into the garbage. She pulls Harper's body to hers by the belt loops of her cut-offs. 'Careful,' Tillie breathes into her. 'You think ya helpin them, but you aint.'

Nineteen, Nineteen and Twenty-One

'Caro's smart,' Harper says. 'She always been smart.'

'I dunno bout that but she try real hard. She's doin good. You gone get yourself back in school?'

'I think so.'

'Good girl. You too good to throw it all away round here with us. How's that taste?'

'It's wonderful. Thanks.'

'Been to see your Mama?'

'Not yet.'

'Wait a while. Settle in for you run over there. You need a rest just much as She does.'

'Caro said yall seen Her.'

Tillie's dress rides up as she crosses her legs and Harper catches a glimpse of the green veins webbing age on her slim thighs. Her skin is stretched taut and yellowing.

'Couple a times.'

'What She say?'

'She miss you.'

'Good,' Harper says.

'You want some more?'

'No m'am, this is plenty. Thank you.'

'Oh sure you do,' Tillie says, already walking into the kitchen again. She shuffles back with a piece of peach cobbler and sets it onto the tray.

'Eat it. Eat it all. When you done, you know where to find her.' She smiles and kisses Harper again.

'She hates the bell.' Caro is lying on her stomach, reading with her arms propped underneath her.

'How's she?' Harper falls into Caro's bed.

'She looks like shit.'

'No she don't—don't say that.'

'Sleeps a lot, doesn't complain much. She's still smoking though.'

'Everybody still smokes but you, Carolyn Naylor.'

'Everybody but me still everything,' Caro says, then pauses. 'But I don't know why she's still doing it. It's like she wants to die or something.'

Harper thinks maybe Tillie wants to die. Because a woman like Tillie isn't afraid to die.

'She don't eat much, do she?'

'Not enough. She says all the pills and shots take away her appetite, but she's still puking all the time even though there's nothing to puke up. She smokes dope when she can get it. It's like living with Collier.' Harper smiles and Caro does too. 'There's this hospital outside of Baltimore with this doctor who gives his patients weed to help them with pain, you know?'

'Yall been up there?'

'Not yet,' Caro says, highlighting a paragraph and flicking the page forward. 'It'll be hard to get up there. She says she doesn't need it but she's a liar. Sometimes she smells like Collier. They both think I'm dumb.'

'Collier get you some of Tommy's.'

'I don't need their help.'

'I'll get you some then.'

'I'd do it myself but if the church found out they'd take away my school money.' Caro stares into the book and Harper watches her fidget with a pen, rolling it back and forth between her fingers. Her hands are stained in bleeding smudges of inkblots. Harper likes how Caro's hands look like they get good use. Ink stamps showing everybody that Caro is working hard at something, showing everybody that Caro is real good at something.

'Whatcha doin then?'

'I can't do anything with you two tonight.'

'I know. Whatcha studyin for?'

'Exam.'

'About what?'

Caro rolls onto her back, throwing her arms open like some debutante Christ. 'Civil War.'

82

There's a small paperback book next to Caro's leg. The cover is dark green with tan and red cursive writing. The author's name sounds like a man, but Harper knows it's a woman.

'You can take it if you want.'

Harper flips through the pages, the words and black type blurring together in a rush. 'Nah.'

'Take it. I'm finished with it. Go ahead and take it. You'll like it. I'd like you to have it.'

Harper thumbs through the pages again. Notes written in blue and red ink are scribbled in the gutter with passages and paragraphs underlined, highlighted and starred.

'There's writin all in it.'

'Yeah, so I don't forget the important parts. And now you won't either.'

Caro dog-eared many of the pages, flagging where she's stopped, stuttered and thought. The inside cover is branded *ENG 356: Modern American Literature*. Harper traces her finger over the permanent marks and smiles, seeing Caro in a real classroom with real people who all read real books. That sort of thing must be real nice. Good for Caro. Caro's earned it.

'You look tired.'

Harper says nothing and tosses the book on the bed.

'Collier's the worst poison there is.'

'Be nice—'

'You should sleep,' Caro says, opening a ragged notebook. 'I'll wake you for dinner.'

Harper nods and then wraps the blue sheets around her body. The mattress gives under her, squeaking as she turns away from Caro and towards the wall. She grabs the book from the foot of the bed and shoves it underneath the sheets with her. Harper opens to the first page: *In the town there were two mutes, and they were always together.*

Used to be I could read Caro's mind by the silence her body spoke. If there was tension between her shoulder blades, or if the web of veins nestled in the crook of her elbow appeared, if her face flushed, I didn't need her words. When I got back, Caro always seemed to be flinching and I never knew why. But her muscles softened and her joints eased when she let Tillie or me hug her or hold her hand. Still, she always seemed to be flinching after she learned how to be good.

And Caro learned how to be good when I left the first time. I'm glad I could do that for her, help her in that way. Caro has eyes so nice and honest that when you look straight into them, you're looking right into her soul. She has a good soul passed down from Tillie and Tillie had the best soul I ever known. Having a good soul means you've got everything sorted with Jesus and that you pay mind to some set of rules. Some rules will kill you though. Some rules will hurt you and make you silent, make you hide and make you sad. Some rules say it's okay when terrible things to happen to you. But other rules not as bad as some folks think—like the rules here.

Here's like prison but with lots more windows and lots less Bibles. The rules here aren't special. No drugs and no drink. Stay clean. Lights out at ten. Don't make a mess and if you do, clean it up. Make your bed every morning and be sure to keep the corners real neat, tucked in tight around the edge of the mattress. Take pride in your appearance and your path to sobriety. No overnight visitors. No smoking inside the house—if you need a smoke, go onto the porch and you best use an ashtray. Do your chores. No locks on the doors because there's nothing to hide here. Do it all. Do all these things or get out.

Lots of nos here. The only thing I've ever been addicted to is saying yes. Yes gets you in trouble and growing up in a place of yes is dangerous. Someone should have told Caro and me and Collier to keep our yeses to ourselves. It was hard to say no when Collier was round. Collier wasn't the type of a girl to say or hear no. It was this real foreign thing to her—the idea she couldn't have something she wanted, do something she wanted *or have who she wanted. She was a girl of yes so she died a girl of yes. The people here are nice enough and try to help with nos. But I'll choke on my nos until I can't breathe no more.*

Everybody keeps to themselves for the most part. I used to hate being alone because of the silence that comes with it. Because being alone means there's nothing to distract you from your own thoughts or from what your body is doing that it shouldn't be doing or isn't doing that it should be doing. Now I like it an awful a lot, being alone. I hate being in crowded rooms with people and eyes and tongues and smiles, people doing nothing but sucking in air just to breathe poison back out again. It used to be that a place wasn't crowded enough for me. Used to be when I was in a room so full with bodies and voices that I couldn't hear the person next to me. Back when there was always plenty of noise so I couldn't hear myself.

Nineteen, Nineteen and Twenty-One

'Why we even come?' Beer leaks from Caro's cup, spilling on the tops of her shoes.

'What?' Harper shouts over the music.

Phil Rankin empties his cup into Harper's. His Washington Bullets jersey is ripped along the collar and a stained white t-shirt pokes out through the sleeves. A fake gold chain holds a fake gold crucifix around his neck. 'Free Harper, right on.'

Tommy's mama's floor is wet with beer and sick. The busted speakers underneath the Burketts' framed family portraits spew banjo-laden riffs while sweaty bodies find each other in kisses, slaps and smiles. Mary-Winston Campbell hooks her hands in Mike's waistband, laughing with her head thrown back as he whispers into her ear. She sways, letting her hips meet his.

'Mary-Winston got fat,' Harper yells. 'She's fat as shit now.'

'She's a fat Melanie Hamilton,' Collier says, balancing three full cups in her hands. Liquid laps against the rims but doesn't spill.

'She wishes she was a fat Melanie Hamilton.' Caro chews on the rim of her cup between swallowing lazy slugs. 'Fuckin pageant trash.'

'Your mama don't like at word, Carolyn.'

'It's weird Charlie's not here.'

'Shut up, Carolyn,' Collier sneers.

'He found him a rich girl now—some girl from D.C. or Baltimore with a dead mama and a rich daddy.'

'Fuck rich girls,' Harper says. 'Where's Tommy at?'

'Over there.'

'Where?'

Tommy's sitting on his mama's couch next to a broken speaker, sucking on a blunt. His mutt, Moses, a stocky brown pit mix nearly blind with glaucoma and lame hind legs from all the fighting Tommy makes him do, sits next to him. Tommy takes a long hit then grabs Moses by the jowls and exhales into his right ear. Moses whimpers, stumbling as his legs catch underneath him. He tumbles from the couch then laps at a small pile of puke on the floor.

'Moses hammered,' Tommy laughs, 'Moses messed up and gone build him the ark now.'

'Noah built the ark,' Caro shouts, across the room. 'Read the Bible, you cracker.'

'Shut up, Caro.'

'You shut up, asshole,' she shouts, giving him the finger.

The room is filled with those Caro and Harper and Collier have loved, hated, and forgotten. They all watch her, their eyes fixed on her flesh, claiming her. Then the looking stops and from their lips silent words spill:

'Hi.'

'Whatever happen to your Mama?'

'Don't even know why they sent you away, not like you killed anybody or nothin.'

'Your Mama dead or what?'

'Your daddy still playin house with your aunt?'

'You ever hear from Charlie? I hear he fuck a rich girl now—'

'What's it like in there?'

'You don't look no different and you don't sound no different neither.'

Harper's pulse is in her throat, her breaths are staccato pants, short, sharp and quick. But she laughs when Collier presses the lit tip of her cigarette to Mary-Winston's shoulder. Mike slips a dirty sandwich bag of his mama's pills into Harper's back pocket then kisses the back of her neck with bourbon slicked lips. Caro shakes her head before she is offered one and Harper shrugs, placing one on her tongue. She uses the cash she swiped from Denise's purse to buy a dime bag off this kid Pete who lives down the block and worked at the Dairy Queen until he got caught rubbing his junk on a stack of cake cones one night after close.

Caro empties and refills her cup four times while Collier and Harper watch, smiling as Caro comes back to them.

In the bathroom Caro's cheeks are so red from her drunk it looks like someone has smacked the life out of her. Pushing past Collier and Harper with her shorts and underwear twisted tight round her knees, Caro squats over the toilet.

'Aint no rush. Stay a while, Caro. Have a seat if you like.' Collier thrusts her mouth under the spigot, letting tap water pour into her mouth.

'I'm not sittin on nothin in this house. Ann-Collier, whatcha catch from Tommy this month?' She sways over the seat, pissing everywhere like some little boy waving his limp self.

'That's disgustin. Sit down, Caro.'

'Just wait till Mike's clap take, you just wait.'

'Where you hide all this sass, Carolyn?' Collier says.

A fist pounds the door. 'Hurry up, we all waitin to go.'

'Go in your mama's mouth, asshole,' Collier shouts.

Caro tries to stand but loses her balance and topples face first into the bathtub, laughing with her shorts and underwear still at her knees.

'Cmon, Caro,' Collier says, pulling her underwear to her hips. 'You all right?'

Caro cackles still.

Collier hikes her skirt up then sits on the toilet seat. 'See what's in there.' She points to the cabinet above the sink.

'Nah, you do it.'

'When you ever said no in your whole entire life, Harper Lucille?' Collier stands and looks down towards the seat. Her blood has marbled in the toilet bowl, just another barren woman. 'Look at that.' Then, real quick, she flicks the tip of her tongue inside Harper's mouth. Harper pushes her away before slapping her across the face.

'I'm so tired of this shit,' Harper says.

Collier brushes the back of her hand across her face and gnaws at her bottom lip. 'I knew you missed it. How long you been itchin for that? You look just like Her, but damn, you meaner, huh?'

And Harper says nothing. 'That's not what I meant—'

'Hear that, Caro? You aint no aunt yet.'

'That's wonderful—' Caro slurs.

Collier grabs a tampon from a torn box in the medicine cabinet then begins twisting all of the small orange bottles label out, towards her, searching for something worth swiping. She grabs four bottles and arranges them in a straight line on the counter. Popping the tops open, she pours four pills from each into her palm before shoving them into her pocket. The memory of the slap already gone.

'Yall want somethin? My treat.'

'Lemme see.'

'Wash your filthy hands, Care-ho.'

'Don't want nothin from you anyways,' Caro says, letting the toilet seat fall as she struggles to button her shorts. She sits, slumping forward with her elbows on her knees, head in her hands.

'Caro, when you gone learn to hold your liquor? Whatcha

want?' Collier says, with a gentle nudge into Harper's ribs. 'Whatcha want?'

'What is it?'

'It matter?'

Harper shrugs.

'She takes them cause they make you not hungry. She takes them cause she aint skinny enough.'

'Give Mary-Winston the whole damn bottle,' Caro shouts.

'—but you just get high and move so fast that there's no time to eat.'

'Yeah, gone then,' Harper says.

Collier spills four fat tablets into her palm then grinds them into the countertop with the pill bottle's lid. She pulls a Chipper Jones card from her back pocket and cuts two fat lines before licking its edge. 'Yall got a dollar?'

Caro tosses a crumpled dollar bill into the sink, which Collier smoothes against her thigh then rolls into a narrow tunnel. Jamming her knuckles into the left side of her nose, she inhales with the dirty bill in her right nostril until the white trail is gone. She snorts and wipes at her nose then hands the dollar to Harper who lowers her head to the sink's edge and does the same.

'Yall a couple of fuckin classy broads,' Caro slurs.

'Your turn, Caro. Just medicine. I'd never let nothing hurt you, princess.'

Caro's eyelids droop like slow falling blinds as Collier pinches a pill between her index finger and thumb and reaches to her.

'Nah, don't.' Caro swats at Collier's hand.

'Gone, it'll wake you up.' She squeezes the hinge of Caro's jaw until a yelp escapes and her mouth pops open. Collier places the pill onto Caro's tongue then forces her lips shut. 'Good Lord, it's just medicine. Swallow, you dummy. Do this in remembrance of me, girl.'

Caro's eyes roll back in surrender. Collier smiles, kisses her on the forehead then unlocks the door. 'Good girl. Your mama be so proud.'

Caro was thirteen and I was thirteen and Collier was fifteen when Tillie got tired of us getting dope sick and shivering in the July heat, so she locked us all in the bathroom with her and made us watch her flush all her pills down the toilet. 'But you need those,' Caro cried. 'You'll rot without them. Stop it.' But Tillie just smiled and flicked her cigarette towards the bathtub. 'Guess I don't need them as much as yall, huh?' Then, she slapped each of us across the face. 'I love you, that's why I keep my hand flat.' First Caro then me and then Collier then Caro four more times.

Funny thing was, Caro never had a taste for any of it, she just like being invited.

Nineteen, Nineteen and Twenty-One
Caro talks real fast about school and people whose names mean nothing to Harper. Caro's life is a bunch of strangers but the communion tablets make Harper listen twice as fast as Caro speaks. She doesn't know what or who Caro's talking about but somehow everything is perfectly clear so she nods then grins, nodding still because Caro seems desperate for it. Caro says she left Collier, returning only in summers, and now she has to pay for it.

'Said why'd we even come?' Caro's hips jut forward with her back arched and shoulder blades against the wall with Tommy's baby pictures and his daddy's favourite buck head.

'Shut up Caro, aint nobody hear you.' Tommy eases himself into her, pushing one hand underneath her shirt and groping between her legs with the other. He laughs when she pushes him away.

'Tommy stop tryin make everybody think yaint a faggot by touchin a pretty girl,' Collier slurs and winks, stumbling into

Caro to kiss her neck. Collier pinches her hip like they're eight and eight and ten again, and Caro laughs because it's the easiest thing to do.

'You know plenty bout faggots, Ann-Collier,' Tommy shouts.

'Gone out back, sweetheart, maybe you find a vein tonight,' Collier says, pressing her palm to Tommy's mouth while smiling the prettiest smile Harper has ever seen.

'You a sloppy bitch,' he says, slapping her arm away and turning towards the mass of people in the living room.

Flesh finds flesh in the dark of Tommy's mama's house because everything feels good when there's no light to cast shadows. Little girls slip in through the back door looking for boys twice their age. 'I been to all your games, seen you play about a million times. My daddy went to high school with your daddy too.' Collier smacks some girl after she watches speed disappear up her nose in the kitchen. The girl can't be more than thirteen and Collier's touch is to warn her, to save her. The girl cries when Collier grabs a handful of her hair and hisses, 'Go home, fuckin slut.'

'—even here for?' Caro says again, her tongue tripping over her words.

'Nothing else t'do.'

'You aint even talkin to no one.'

'I talk to you, don't I?' Harper says.

Collier lets Tommy's hands fumble against her flesh in an apology by the stereo. With her head titled back, neck to the stucco ceiling and her weight against the wall with his weight on her, she touches him like she's supposed to. Touches him like Harper and Caro have always seen her do. Collier's eyes lazily shut every few seconds and it's hard to tell if she's even conscious. But Tommy wouldn't care either way.

'They so gross,' Caro slurs, 'he so gross. I'm sorry—you know, with him and that shit Collier let happen, it wouldn't have happened if I had been there, I swear—'

'Shut up, Caro.'

91

Tommy's daddy's front lawn is crowded with beat-up Fords parked and paying no mind to the grass and tulips trying to grow. The front door bursts open and Gabe Wells starts pissing before he's finished unzipping his pants. Harper pulls the sandwich bag and papers from her back pocket and begins rolling.

'Could you like,' Caro hiccups, 'go back for this?'

Harper drops three fat pinches into the paper and gently rolls the skin back and forth. 'Aint never lost it—She be so proud.'

'You break parole every day, you'll get caught sooner or later.'

'Nah, I'm a lucky girl.'

'Not half as lucky as your Mama is. You flush it out before you test?'

'Yeah, Collier'll give me somethin. You worry too much. You didn't used to be like this, shakin and flinchin all the time.'

'What if someone see us?'

'Quit it—it don't matter.'

'Course it do. What if someone catch us?'

'No one will unless you a snitch.'

'Shut up, I aint no snitch.' Caro laughs with one of those cackles that start real deep in the pit of your stomach. Laughing so hard your insides coil tight and cramp. When Caro smiles, she looks just like Tillie, but healthy.

'You wanna go?'

'What? Go where?' Harper says, licking the paper's edge. 'You okay?'

'Yeah.' Caro lays on her back with her hands above her head.

'This gone make you sick? You gone get the spins?' Harper holds the lighter to the tip of the joint and red embers flare as she inhales. 'You gone puke, Carolyn?'

'No,' she says, a smile spreading slowly across her face.

'Collier say you too busy for her now. Where you been?'

'She's the worst.'

'She say you don't come out here no more. She said you look sad all the time and kill her buzz.'

'I'm sad cause I know the reasons I hate her are the same reasons you love her. And know what else? Reason I don't come out here no more is cause I hate it out here.'

'We didn't have to come,' Harper says, handing the joint to Caro.

'Course we did.' Caro takes a long hit then breathes a mouthful of blue smoke into the air. 'How long can a person do the same stupid stuff and act like it's a life? Can I ask you somethin?'

'Yeah, gone then.'

'You made her look worse. How'd you make Collier look worse?'

'Worse than what?' The smoke fills Harper's lungs and throat and mouth and she's thinking that suffocating can't be as bad as most people make it out to be.

'Dunno, just worse I guess,' Caro says. 'But she needs to stop.'

'Stop what?' Harper tilts her head up, shuts her right eye and exhales a spiral towards the moon.

'Stop everythin. Harper—'

'What?'

'I'm glad you're out. And Harper—'

'What?'

'Your Mama aint even here no more—you so stupid for comin back. There aint no cure for whatever Collier and your Mama got, they aint got no choice but to act like assholes. My mama says you're different.'

Harper says nothing and takes another hit, holding the breath deep inside her where no one can touch or see it. 'What's your mama say about you then?'

'She says I aint as smart as you are and if I want people to think I'm smart as I pretend to be, I better work harder. So I do.'

'Where else would I go?'

'I wish I could have gone too.'

'You must be some type a hammered to be sayin such stupid shit.'

'Collier should have gone—but your Mama the one who should have gone the most.' Caro takes the joint from Harper and lays back into the bed of dead grass. 'But I wish I could have gone too.'

'You a real ball to hang round with now.' Harper still looks up with her right eye shut. 'And I tell ya what, you don't wish that—you think you do, but ya don't.'

'You shouldn't have come back here.'

'You wastin a high, you know that?'

'You wastin a high, you know that?' Caro mimics, smiling. 'Wanna burn this place to the ground. I will too—watch me, one day I'll come back, torch it.'

Harper takes the joint before ripping handfuls of grass and tossing them towards her feet. The sharp edges of dead earth prick her hands.

'Why don't you tell me nothin no more?' Caro says.

'I do too.'

'You so quiet now,' Caro says, pinching hard at the skin of her knees. She'll have bruises by sunrise. 'I hate it.'

'I tell you somethin when I got somethin to tell.'

'I'm sorry I didn't tell you bout Charlie leavin.'

'You drunk on your sorrys tonight, huh?'

'More sad than I am sorry.'

'A glass of water and a slap will help you not feel sorry.'

'Shut up.'

'What makes you sad?' Harpers says.

'I get sad when I think about Collier droppin Job. I get sad when I think about hearin his head hit the floor and how I heard it even though I was in the hall and how I bet your Mama heard it too but didn't do nothin about it. I think about it all, lots.'

'Me too.'

'Collier do too.'

'Don't nobody have a clue what she think about,' Harper says, 'don't nobody know what happens in her head.'

'Uh huh, she told me while back. And every time she sees him she touches his head real soft. Watch her. She do. She touches him like—like if she does it long enough he'll forgive her or somethin. She miss your Mama too, know how much she like when your Mama walk around without no shirt on.'

'She never tried,' Harper says, 'She always too thirsty to dress Herself is all.'

'She didn't know no better.'

'That so?'

'She tried. Nobody helped Her, but She tried. That's what my mama says.'

'Your mama's a liar then.'

'My mama said you allowed to be mad.'

Harper says nothing, squinting in the dark and digging her fingernails into the earth.

'She says you allowed to be mad cause of what Collier did to us and what your daddy went and done to your Mama. He shouldn't have done what he did. My mama said he's going to hell for it. She said she prays every night that he dies. And she prays every night for you and your Mama. But Collier was the saddest when your daddy let them take Her.'

'Collier as lazy as she is stupid.'

'Don't be jealous, you still her favourite. Collier still have you.'

'Say somethin else. I'd love nothin more than to pop you in the mouth, Carolyn.'

Caro takes the nub from Harper's lips and shoves it into the ground with a near silent hiss. 'Don't call me that, it aint the name she gave me. Hate when yall call me that and I hate—I hate that things happened to you that didn't happen to me.'

'We never been the same, Caro.'

95

'We used to be—used to be everythin that happened to you, happened to me.'

Fifteen, Fifteen and Seventeen

With her knees pulled into her chest, forehead resting on her crossed arms, Harper sees nothing but Caro who's bleeding and sweating and praying and sober.

'The hell happen now, Harper?' A fat finger pokes her shoulder then snaps the bra strap peeking out from underneath her shirtsleeve. 'You look at me now.'

Tommy's daddy, Bart, stands over her, his broad frame blocking sunlight from her face. His dull badge and gun hang limp in his shadow. Caro stares into the pavement because she can't bring herself to look anywhere but down. They are trapped in the shade of Bart's sheriff's car, the county name plastered on the side in white stickers.

Bart reaches for Harper's face but she jerks away, moving closer to Caro. Neighbours stand in the grass lining the concrete limbs of the intersection. A row of parked cars with blinking hazards and the tow truck and the kids with backpacks and Her accordioned car hood are all still and paralyzed. Caro's already puked a bunch of times and has no more sick to get up so she dry heaves between her knees until her body stops shaking.

'We gotta go—get Collier,' Harper says. 'Aint nobody gone be there when she done.'

Bart laughs, spitting a mouthful of dip into a Pepsi can. Tobacco drips from his beard onto the toe of Harper's shoe. She picks at the darkest shade of a scab on her elbow and Caro swats at her hand.

'Don't, it'll scar.'

'Sweetheart, Ann-Collier Ward the least of your problems. Now, tell me what happen.'

'Suck a dick, old man.'

Bart crouches behind the driver's side door blocking the view of passersby and rubberneckers, snatches his gun from its holster and brings its butt down into Harper's forehead. The skin splits open and her face seeps blood, her own mixing with Caro's dried handprint from before. Caro shoves her trembling hand into her pocket and offers Harper a dirty tissue. She takes it and tries to pull away but Caro won't let go.

'Best watch at mouth, young lady,' he says, spewing a brown jet at her feet. Bart points the gun towards Harper with a loose wrist. It bobs in his right hand, beating down on his slow, easy syllables. 'Awful quiet now. Your daddy gone love this one, huh?' He kneels in front of Caro. Taking off his glasses, he traces his thumb from her earlobe to her chin. She cries harder, says nothing.

'You much prettier when you smile, Carolyn Naylor.' She flinches but keeps her eyes on the concrete, not giving him the privilege of looking into her. 'Ya know, you girls plain retarded. You gone tell me what happen? Why you in your daddy's car?'

'It aint his car,' Harper says, still holding Caro's hand.

'This your Mama's car? This your Mama's car means the things in it Hers? You got any idea what I found in the dashboard, Harper?'

'Whatever it is, sure you put it there.'

'Keep runnin your mouth and I'll cut that tongue clean out it—you hear me, girl?'

Harper says nothing and Caro says nothing.

'Now, I know it's your Mama's but speak up, girl, if you got somethin to say. You best save yourself. They gone drag Her ass away on this shit—put Her where she belong, so if you got somethin to say you best do it now.'

Caro pukes like she prays, spilling her guts until she has nothing left and Harper watches, knowing she won't always be like this, with blood and sick drying on her skin, tremors pulsing through her limbs she writes like trash no one can even read this Caro I don't like that kinda talk be polite you the smart one Caro She had said She don't fix dinner when She's tired and She's just tired is all needs someone to hug Her is all.

'It's mine,' Harper says.

Caro shakes her head making no noise with her eyes hard and her mouth wet, her face soaked in tears and snot and vomit and blood. And then Caro starts praying loud enough for Harper and God to hear.

'What's yours?'

'The bag—the bag in the dash. It's mine,' Harper says and Harper says and then she says nothing.

A red car races around the corner, comes to a quick halt behind the tow truck and burning rubber fills Harper's lungs. The driver's side door opens, the car still running, and Harper's daddy runs to her. She thinks she'll puke but nothing comes up. Caro puts her hand on Harper's back and she hasn't stopped praying.

'What happen?' Luke whispers. His face is real close to hers but they're not touching. His face is so close that for the first time she sees why people think he could be her brother instead of her daddy.

'Dunno.'

'Don't be smart, stop actin like Her. Tell me what happen,' he says.

Bart returns the sunglasses to his face and gives the butt of the gun a quick wipe on the leg of his pants.

'Dunno—just, just did it for a second. Honest. Just a second, sometimes She lets me do it to the store if She too tired,' Harper says.

'I swear to Christ, Harper—'

Caro's crying still but no sounds come out. She bows her head lower and shuts her eyes when she finally breathes, 'Amen.'

'Just tired is all,' Harper says. 'We have to go get Collier—'

'Tired huh?' Bart says. 'That why you need two grand of dope—cause you tired?'

'Didn't do nothin wrong,' Harper says to no one.

Bart clips the cuffs onto her wrists, pulling Harper's body to his. The metal is heavy and cuts into her skin. Her knees buckle and he yanks the cuffs harder to resurrect her bones. Harper rises.

'Where's she goin?' Caro stands and makes a fist around the cuff of Harper's right hand. Luke unlocks her grip to push Caro's body away from the road.

'Collier better thank Christ every day the rest of her life she aint here.'

Bart pulls Harper by her wrists to the cage in the back then tosses the dirty bladder of pills onto the front seat before slamming the passenger side door.

'I'll send her Mama for her,' Luke calls, walking to his car.

Turning onto the main road, Harper watches Caro standing in the middle of the street crying without anybody to hold her hand.

Nineteen, Nineteen and Twenty-One
Matt Shifflett staggers from the front door to the edge of the driveway then pisses into a pile of mulch.

'Can I ask you somethin else?' Caro speaks different sometimes, speaks like she used to, speaks like she should. Her vowels get long when she drinks more than she should. Words pour from her mouth in a gentle, syrupy slur, with a Valley drawl like her mama. And when Caro's has too much to drink, she speaks in slack-jawed contradictions and her eyes go glassy. Like the rest of them. Like the rest of the prisoners. She talks like she's from here. Harper likes it even though she shouldn't because liking it will just hurt Caro. And Caro doesn't belong here anymore.

'You full a questions tonight.'

'So?' Caro says.

Harper smiles. 'Gone then.'

'She asked you, she didn't ask me.'

'That aint a question.'

'I would have done it. She doesn't think so, but I would have.'

'That aint a question either,' Harper says. 'Ask me a question.'

'When you was with, when you with Collier other day—'
She speaks like Tillie and talks herself in circles making Harper dizzy. 'When you with Collier other day—'

'Yeah,' Harper says, lying next to her in the grass.

'Other day,' Caro begins again, having lost her place, '—other day, you hit her in the face. I could tell.'

'You got a cigarette?'

'You hit her with your hand?'

'You got cigarettes or not?'

'When you hit her the other day, other day in the woods, what you hit her with?' Caro asks again.

'With a bottle.'

'Why's it always a bottle?'

'Cause it is.'

'So you—so when you hit her, so when you hit Collier other day in the woods with a bottle, Harper—'

'You even listenin to me? Askin the same question fifty times?' She thinks about rolling another joint but doesn't because Caro's eyes lazily roll back into her head like an exhausted slot machine.

'What it feel like?' Caro finally says.

And Harper says nothing.

'Sometimes I wonder if I'll even cry at Collier's funeral. I'm scared I won't. Can't help it—but promise me, promise me when we there, promise me at if I aint cryin you do somethin to make me.'

Harper looks into her, squints past her own drunk and looks into Caro. 'Like what?' she says, smiling at Caro because she needs the help.

'Dunno, maybe like—could like stab me or somethin.'

Harper laughs hard in a way she hasn't in a real long time. Caro's so pathetic and simple looking in the dark and Harper keeps laughing real hard.

'It's not funny. Don't gotta be a stab, just that a pinch aint hard enough. We think a somethin though—just, just promise me.'

'I'll do it for you, if you do it for me. What make you think we be at hers and she aint gone be at ours?'

'She'll die first. You know she will. She knows it too,' Caro says.

'How you know that?'

'Every day Collier wakes up, she dares God to kill her. Soon or later, He gone take her up on it.'

'What if she at ours? What if Collier and you at my funeral? What you gone do then?'

'I'd cry at yours. I already did.' Caro is lying on her back, looking blankly towards the sky with her hands behind her head—like she's praying to forget where and who she is. 'You know everything there is to know about me.'

'Same.'

'Used to be but not no more.'

'You shouldn't smoke no more,' Harper says, reaching for an abandoned cup in the grass. She smells it then steals the last four swallows. 'Whatcha lookin for, Carolyn? Hope yaint looking for angels. Aint no angels around here, not a single one cause we got witches instead.'

'Shut up,' Caro says, smiling. 'My mama don't like at kinda talk either.'

'Gone then, Caro, ask me what you can't durin daylight.'

Caro struggles to sit. Her face pale and sweaty and she'll vomit soon. Caro steadies herself, crosses her legs and sits up real straight. 'You like, fight anyone or anythin? You kill anyone?'

'Not yet.'

'That aint funny.'

'It's a stupid question. Course I haven't. I kill Tommy before I kill a stranger.'

'They mean to you?'

'What?'

'Anyone like, ever make you do stuff you didn't wanna?'

101

'At first.'

'At first what?'

'At first I didn't want to,' Harper says, looking straight up into the clear night. She shuts her right eye again and stares towards the moon, not knowing what she was aiming for. 'Then after a while I guess I did.'

'Why?'

'Made it easy.'

'You tell Collier things ya don't tell me and I hate it.'

'No I don't.'

'Collier ask you the things I do?'

'Only thing Collier ask me for is money,' Harper says.

'How'd it feel?'

'How'd what feel?'

'Everythin?' Caro wipes sweat from her face with her scarred palm. 'How everythin make you feel?'

'I dunno yet.'

'Sorry you went alone.' Caro's voice trails into the dark and her tongue finally slows as she shuts her eyes and passes out. Sleeping, she's safe.

We wasted time to waste it, waiting for things to happen to us. I learned lots from Caro and Collier in the summers. They taught me things to pass the time because being bored could be a sin if you was bored enough. That night—after Caro passed out in the grass and I had to drag her home best I could and fling her into bed without waking Tillie—you only get drunk when you stop drinking. Bad things only happen when you stop drinking, not when you are. You only start running your mouth when it's quiet.

Took a long time to walk home from Caro's that night. I emptied my pockets into my mouth so that it felt like the ground was shifting under me with each step. I learned that no matter where you're coming from, it takes a real long time to get home whether you want to get there or not.

Thirteen, Thirteen and Fifteen

'Yalls Mamas gettin high again,' Collier says, grasping a low hanging branch with her soles brushing the ground. A cigarette hangs from the corner of her mouth and she pumps her legs, the branch rubbing her palms raw as daylight fades. 'But I aint never been half as messed up as She gets.'

'She don't *get* anythin,' Harper says, her tongue still tasting ripe cherry flesh, 'She just is.'

They stand at the furthest corner of Caro's backyard, swiping at the cherry tree's heaviest limbs, watching Tillie and Luce split a joint and bottles of spiked Coke. Tillie's lips move quickly in distant whispers and when she places her palm on the crown of Luce's head, gently pulling Her in, they laugh and laugh and laugh with their mouths wide open, offering their throats to the sunset. Harper watches them in silence knowing she'll never share those secrets.

Caro grabs hold of the weakest branch and swings like a skinny pendulum towards the fence with rusting wire knots, then away. Her arms peel in a sunburned rot. White flaps of dead skin fold back from her pink flesh, but they aren't nearly as busted up as her legs.

'Damn, Caro—your legs real torn up.'

Fresh scabs claim last week's beating. Crusted and healing lashes cross and overlap on the backs of Caro's knees and thighs. Harper counts each slash and stops at twelve.

'She's stronger than she used to be,' Caro says. 'Stop swipin her pills, assholes. I'll die with my legs like this—I'm so tired of gettin switched for yall.'

'Shut up, Caro, you had just as many as we did. Not my fault my Mama too tired to hit me no more.'

'I love them both more than my own mama,' Collier says, tossing a handful of cherry pits over the fence.

Harper says nothing, just stares at Collier's sun-bleached hair hanging in greasy strings hiding her hard eyes, with her arms and legs covered in goose bumps.

'Yeah, but you didn't even come out of Donna, sides she a piece a trash anyways so that don't mean nothin,' Caro says.

'I guess.'

A gust of hot air spins the patriotic pinwheel Caro shoved into the earth a month ago. The cherry tree grows taller at sunset, casting shadows that swallow their bodies and cool their skin. Harper presses her back into the tree trunk letting dry bark brand her while Tillie and Luce spark cigarettes and laugh.

'You rather get shot or get stabbed?' Luce asks with lungs full of smoke and a pocket bloated with Tillie's pills.

'Stabbed—I could live through a stabbin.' Harper walks heel to toe along the double yellow lines with her arms outstretched.

'At so?'

'Yeah—I got a body for stabbin.'

'Damn right you do.' Luce's face is shining with booze and sweat and laughter. 'You better hope so—you better hope you got what I got.' She ashes the cigarette then hands the bourbon-spiked backwash of the bottle to Harper. Draining it slow, tasting Her lips and Her words and the secrets she doesn't know in the sweet kick of Her favourite poison, Harper swallows.

'Your turn.'

'I dunno,' Harper says, 'I can't never think of good ones.'

'Cmon.' She gently palms Harper's skull then shakes it.

'Alright—you uh, you rather me get murdered or Job?'

She takes a long pull then exhales a thick strip of smoke above her head. 'Job—I rather Job get murdered if it means you live, if it means I keep you.'

'He's just a little boy is all,' Harper says.

'There's worse things in the world than losin a little boy.'

'Like what?'

'Like losin a little girl,' She says.

Even in the dark, Her angles are illuminated. Beautiful, free and loose, Her smile kinder than the morning's. After sunset, She is the light.

'Only thing God ever done for me was give me you.' The cigarette's glowing embers set Her gaze aflame. 'Our kind run heavy with girls—Job a mistake. He'll know it one day.'

The soles of their tennis shoes beat the street in dry slaps. Harper overhands the empty bottle down the street and it shatters in the dark.

'You so quiet.'

Harper says nothing.

'I don't like it when you so quiet.'

'Why?'

'I like the things you say and how you say them.'

Harper scoffs, taking the cigarette from Her fingers and brings it to her own lips.

'Quiet ones the dangerous ones. I don't like quiet. Nothin good come from quiet.'

'What do You and Tillie talk about?'

'What? When?'

'Always.'

'Secrets,' She hisses, pressing Her lips to Harper's forehead.

'Tell me.'

'No.'

'Why not then?'

'Make your own secrets, girl—yaint got no use for mine.'

'I wanna know Yours.'

'Not tonight you don't.'

'Yours the only ones I wanna know,' Harper says.

'Make your own. Filthy ones, ones that make you strong. Make them with Caro and Collier—that's why God gave them to you.'

'Why me?'

'Prolly cause He wants you to save them.'

'You tell Collier things You don't tell me.'

'You don't need to hear the same things Collier do. They

105

found you—God gave them to you cause He want you to have secrets without me. You can have whatever secrets you want, girl, just don't get caught.'

Harper turns to her daddy's house, striding towards the driveway.

'Hey,' She calls, still standing in the middle of the street. 'Let's keep goin.'

'Why? We're home.'

'I aint done walkin yet. Cmon, we aint done.'

'I'm tired.'

'Let's keep goin.'

'Why?'

'You wanna hear a secret?' She yells, walking backwards towards the flow of invisible traffic, down the street in the dark.

I never breathed a single word She told me. I let Her secret sit on my tongue until I finally had the courage to swallow it down but it didn't stay down and I couldn't keep it in my belly because I started coughing and choking on Her words until I puked it all up. The next morning I was so tired I could barely stand but I couldn't stop staring at Her. Her words from the night before simmered in my head while I sat on the back porch until sunset asking God what I should think and what I should do because no one would tell me.

There's a difference between what was and what wasn't—a doctor told me that once. You can't just pick and choose what happened and what didn't, what you remember and what you forget. But he didn't know what he was talking about and I know for sure that summer was nothing but time and sweat and thirst and cherry trees, Tillie's cigarette butts and the stink of trash and flesh that the wind carried into our mouths. And I know for sure that there's no reason to name someone who's never breathed but I figure our sister would have been called something beautiful like Elizabeth and she would have looked like me and hated our daddy just as much as I did.

Nineteen, Nineteen and Twenty-One

He keeps the front door unlocked, day and night. Stupid old man. That's how people get killed. Don't he know that's how people get killed? It's barely sunrise and Harper slams the door behind her then trips over Job's untied cleats.

'Keep it down,' her daddy says, sitting in his chair slowly rocking. It's dark except for the orange pulse of his cigarette. He sits there smoking and rocking.

With booze heavy limbs dead and extended, she lies face down on the couch and lets her feet hang over the edge. Dried clumps of mud from her soles fall onto the floor.

'Know what time is?' he says.

'I dunno what day it is, old man.'

'Quarter after five in the mornin.'

'Shouldn't smoke—poison'll kill you, old man.'

'So I heard,' he says.

'Why aintcha sleep? Whatcha up for?'

'Been wonderin where my kid gone.'

'Well—suppose your kid, suppose he in bed like all good little boys. How you even know he yours?'

'Where you been, girl?' he asks.

Harper says nothing.

'Who you been with?'

Harper says nothing.

'You with Collier? Collier get you like this.'

'No sir.'

'You lyin to me?'

'Yessir—yessir, I'm lyin to you. Yessir, I am.'

'You pick a fight only half good as your Mama did.' He stubs his cigarette straight into the coffee table and quickly lights another. 'Still got time to learn, don't you, girl? Yaint dead yet, huh?'

'Hope your girlfriend don't catch you smokin in her house.'

'You stink, you know that? You smell like your Mama. You beggin to go back? Hell's wrong with you? Whatever the hell it is, aint from my side. I know that for damn sure, little girl.'

'Nothin's wrong with me, sir. Aint no little girl neither.'

'Sure is, you sure is a little girl if I ever seen one.'

He wants to cock back and sock her in the mouth, Harper tastes it. She feels how bad he wants it. Hears him chewing on the dry cigarette, gnawing the white body and grinding the filter between his wide and crooked teeth.

'You sure is and you want to know why? Cause you just like that Mama of yours. Runnin around doin whatever the hell you please, not thinkin bout nobody else, not thinkin there are other people tryin to get by, tryin to live in the hurricane you and Her is. But it aint just you. You a little girl cause you still think, like at Mama of yours do, that you gone live forever.'

Harper says nothing.

'You look just like Her. You know that? Comin in here five in the mornin, smellin like your Mama. That's why you so proud, huh? It's like She's here right now, just like it used to be—Luce stumblin round, laughin, sayin the things She too scared to say in the daylight. Only time She proud is in the dark.'

'She proud of what come out of Her?' Harper says.

Sunlight breaks in the distance, nearly a full county over, and pours through the window. She can make out the things that fill the living room. Books and baseballs and newspapers and matchbox cars and candy cigarette boxes and the things Job will throw out soon.

'Don't know what She thinks,' he says, 'never have. I don't know what goes on in that goddam head of Hers.'

'I bet—' Harper says, pushing herself up from the couch, 'I bet—I know, She hate you. For what you done to Her, where you made Her go. She don't need to be there. You the one made Her tired, you the one made Her sad. I'm so glad it's dark. You wanna know why? We can't stand the sight of you.'

He leans forward, placing his face into his hands. Harper waits. Harper waits for him to rear his fist back and bring it

108

straight into her. Break her nose, knock her teeth loose, bust her eye socket open and blind her, box her ears until they spit a river of Her blood down her neck, kick her in the stomach, in the throat. Harper waits for him to leave his mark on her—something to help her remember that he's her daddy and he has to care, even if he doesn't want to. Even if he gave up a long time ago. She never did that and She never will and She never gave up on Harper.

'You think you know Her, but you don't,' he says.

'Yeah, I do—course I know my own Mother.'

'Naw girl, you don't. You don't know what She really like. You don't know Her nature.'

'I do so. Know Her better than anyone ever. Know She wouldn't go and lay with your brothers if you was gone.'

He laughs and presses the half-smoked cigarette into the table. 'You be mighty surprised things She gone and done.'

'You need to shave, you look like trash.'

His smile settles into the blunt creases framing his mouth. His face says nothing and his eyes say nothing as he runs a hand slowly over his head. He won't look at Harper now, just bends over his knees, staring at the floor. 'What I do wrong, girl? You tell me. What I do wrong to girls like you and Her?'

Harper inhales as her head swells with Collier's communion. It burns still, spinning inside her brain and she wonders if she really is his. And her mind turns faster. She thinks nothing because thinking about nothing is easier than looking at him as sunrise spills over his face highlighting the wrinkles she's given him and the blotched patchy skin from his old tears. Harper does this because it's easy. She does things because they're easy and they make her feel good. 'She hate me too?'

'No.' He places the cigarette pack into his pocket and for the first time she sees he's looking right at her.

'Do you?' she says.

'Do I what?'

'You hate me?'

They're gazing at each other now, into each other. He stands and he looks the same in the dark as he does in the light. 'You look just like Her—lucky girl.' Heavy footsteps take him into the kitchen to fill a glass with tap water. He rattles a bottle of aspirin and returns to her.

'You been pillin?'

'No sir.'

'Don't—you been pillin or not? Only get these if you aint had nothin else.'

'I said I haven't.'

'Take these and go to bed, sleep it off. That's one thing She taught you.' He offers her a palm of three aspirin. 'And listen—you got to change them clothes, all right? Have a wash and put on somethin clean. I mean it. It's weeks you been wearin this shit now. You stink and you look like trash. Hey, you hear me?'

Harper takes his hand in hers before grabbing the pills, feeling the rough skin of his dry palms, his split and battered knuckles. 'I'm gonna feel—' she hiccups, 'I'm gonna feel sick tomorrow.'

'Girl, it is tomorrow. You get sick, better be in the toilet. Hey, you hear me?' He shakes his hand from her grip and his arm drops. It's just light enough to see his scar. When he was a little boy and tripped over a pile of snow-covered firewood, falling face first on a pickaxe. Gave him a three-inch cut above his right eye. He saw blood for weeks, Harper's granny had told her, he could have been blind, your daddy. He could have gone blind but he didn't. But maybe it would have been better if he had gone blind because he never would have seen Her.

'What if I don't?' Harper says, 'What if I don't make it? Sometimes I don't.'

'You will. You better. You get sick better be sick before church. I mean it. Last thing I need is you causin a scene again. You hear me?'

'It's okay if you hate me,' she says.

110

He breathes tobacco into her ear. 'You hate me?'
'Nope.' And she's the best liar of them all.
'I'm sorry,' he says.
She knows he's lying. She doesn't care.

He just sat there at daybreak with his head bowed. Don't know what for, but I wish he would have cried. Never seen a man cry. Never known a man who gave himself the chance I guess. He didn't hit me and he didn't yell because I am the living 'Told you so' he always wanted to give Her but never had the chance to. Sometimes when he looked at me, I could see him asking himself when the last time he had Her was before I was born. But looking at me he wasn't mad at Her, he was happy because if I'm not his, then nothing's his fault. It's all Hers. It's Her blood and who She is. Everything is Hers. I am the flesh, I am Her flesh. But no matter who you come from, there are just some things you can't rid yourself of no matter how much you puke or pray. And sometimes there are things you can't shake off because even though you say you don't want them, deep down you do.

Most people here don't know about Her. But I told Jenny a little one day after group. 'She sounds like, real sexy—like one them dirty actresses from the sixties. Those actresses with the real smoky voices and real thin bodies who be sucking cigarettes and drinking champagne all the time. Your Mama, she have nice tits? Or you and your brother suck her dry?'

Never heard him talk about Her after that night. Not once in my life heard him talk about what Her voice sounded like to him, or how they met because She asked him for a light, or what made him want Her so bad—or how his daddy forced him to propose when She started swelling with me. I don't know what happen after I came out of Her. Never asked Her and never asked him and never asked nobody since I never wanted to know.

Don't hate him. Don't hate him because he hates himself

plenty on his own. He's awful pathetic and needs lots of love to keep him going cause he's barely a man at all. He's a sad old man, so don't hate him. His sin is that he loves wild wild women. Don't hold that against him because he's desperate. And a desperate man is the worst kind of man there is. He is. Don't let him or nobody else tell you different. But don't hate him, I hate him plenty for the both of us, every day.

Nineteen, Nineteen and Twenty-One

'Get back up there,' he says. His charcoal suit hangs on him like a dead and wrinkled skin. 'You look like sin.' He stands over a pan, running a fork through broken egg yolks while Denise gently brushes against him every chance she steals.

'Don't got nothin to wear,' Harper says.

'Course you do.'

'Don't fit in nothin up there.'

'Well, just gotta watch what you eat then, honey.' Denise hooks a finger into one of his belt loops, pulling him to her and handing him a plate of toast.

'Don't fit cause I aint fourteen no more, now am I?'

'Give it a rest, Harper.'

'Gone grab somethin of mine, honey. Somethin of mine will make you look real nice.' Denise winks at Harper as she sets the table for three, not four.

Suffocating in Denise's sequins and tattered cotton dresses shoved into the racks and shelves, Luke's shirts and ties hang slack, waiting to slip and collect on the floor. But in the back corner hangs one of Hers, thin and transparent. Draped from a wire hanger, it's lifeless.

She peels her shirt and shorts from her flesh, shedding sweaty fabric skins. Taking the white eyelet dress from its hanger, Harper lets Her limp layer rest on her arm. The fabric's scent is dank and flat and has a moth eaten hem. She unzips the dress, steps into it and lets the material meld into her. The white cloth makes Harper's skin look soiled at the hinges of her elbows and knees where her filth stains darker. Grabbing cigarettes from the nightstand, Harper lights one and smokes in front of the mirror, letting it catch Her dirty reflection. She drapes her left arm across her stomach, props her right elbow steady and lets her hand hang palm up with the cigarette laced between her fingers. She takes long drags and exhales thin spirals towards the ceiling. She watches Her smoke in the mirror, she watches herself.

'Harper,' Denise yells from downstairs. 'Harper, you smokin up there? Put it out I said. Don't be smokin in your daddy's house now.'

Harper stares close with her face pushed to the glass. Looking into her black pupils with their exhausted grey flecks, Harper sees Her clearer than she ever has. Like they all tell her, her Mother's daughter. They all say it. They do.

'You look nice,' her daddy says, standing in the living room while Denise tightens his tie.

'Yeah, thanks.'

'Yeah, nice.' Job barrels down the stairs behind her, his shirt and jacket unbuttoned with a crumpled and sweat-stained tie flung around his neck.

'Cmon, that's enough, we late as it is,' Denise says, dragging her sharp-heeled hooves across the floorboards and leaving shallow scars in her wake.

Harper's daddy wears a necktie and jacket even though it's hotter than ninety degrees out and not even ten in the morning. Job is dressed in clothes that make him fidget against his body, make him hate his own skin. Denise wears no jewelry and no neon shades. Just black.

Sweaty faces clutter the sanctuary. Clothes melt into damp skin. Dust has never been able to settle in this Holy room but

113

somehow it's always musty. The women wear ankle length dresses in the sweltering heat and fan themselves with creased bulletins that report times and locations of Sunday school classes, fundraisers, potluck dinners and next month's union between Mark Reynolds and Susie Palmer. But these women aren't women at all, just girls with more wrinkles than before. Before they were broken of their bad habits. But these women, these women wearing silk gloves sweat through the fabric veiling their bodies. These are the women who forget the heat and forget the season. Limp-brimmed hats cover the gnawed, sunburned and aging flesh of their faces.

The men watch her. They are all failed somethings—failed athletes, failed politicians, failed preachers, failed blues guitarists. Lazy daddies. They hide underneath their three button blazers, the cloth masking their stink of fried diners, burnt coffee grinds and Saturday city nights. Sunday mornings the sanctuary washes them anew, baptizes them in good boy innocence. But the minute they step into the street, they remember where they are and Satan claims them. This valley has a floor lined with the defeat of half-dead boys.

Bart sits with his army of broken brothers in the opposite pew. Wearing a cheap grey suit and a cheap white shirt and a cheap expression, he's not one bit different. He catches her eye and winks. Tobacco trails down his chin after he spits into a Pepsi bottle and Harper squeezes her thighs together as tight as she can.

Harper and Job and Luke and Denise sit shoulder to shoulder. The gaze of all the men and all the women settle on Harper, on Her dress, on her unwashed hair and flushed chest, on her body that's still leaking poison. Harper watches her daddy watching the men and the women. He pulls at the cuff of his left sleeve, trying to cover the tattoo on his forearm—his abomination to the Lord, adorning his body with ink, glorifying himself. *Ye shall not make nay cuttings in your flesh for the dead, nor print any marks upon you: I am the LORD*. The initials of his mama are fading but still laced into that blue anchor. He was never in the Navy and he never loved his mama.

'People starin,' Harper says to no one.

'Shhh,' Denise wheezes, 'Aint all about you. Jesus, you always think everythin about you.'

On the far side of the sanctuary, Tillie sits with Caro who can barely keep her eyes open. Her head nods back and forth and Tillie rolls her eyes when she has to pinch Caro's side to wake her up. Tillie drapes a blue shawl across her shoulders, shielding her frame. Caro's pale pink sundress is wrinkled and her hair hangs in a greasy curtain across her face, across last night's sin. Desperate for sleep, with her spine hunched, she makes no effort to unveil her face. When she finally wakes, Caro fans herself with a crumpled church bulletin just like one of them. Just like one of the women. Harper watches her wondering if it's the first time Caro has been one of them, or if it's just the first time she's noticed.

Pastor Jim walks along the aisles, shaking hands and wearing the special smile he saves for Sundays. He keeps his coal-coloured hair slicked back with cheap shoeshine and his seersucker suit cut close to his body. He wears twenty-four carat gold cufflinks and touches them, first the left one then the right, at each and every mention of tithing.

Harper's daddy knew Jim Nichols back when he was just a puny kid stealing sips, spliffs and gropes underneath the bleachers at football games. Jimmy Nichols found the Lord after the police swept up the ashes of his girlfriend in a cooking fire he claimed he knew nothing about. Harper's daddy says Pastor Jim hates queers because he is one.

They speak to no one. They sit in silence. Harper's daddy gently pats Denise's bare knee. Job loosens the navy tie, sloppy and barely knotted around his neck. His shirttails hang over his belt and the knees of his khaki trousers are painted in long set grass stains. Denise licks her palm and smears it against

Job's untamed cowlick. He jerks away, moving closer to Harper and presses his body against hers. He's simple and wonderful in the wreckage of his Sunday best.

'Denise says it's trashy to come to church drunk cause God hates that kinda thing.'

'Maybe she should read the Old Testament then,' Harper says.

The eyes of the men and the women and the people sit heavy on her skin. The room has no circulation, just the flat, musty breaths of the congregation. The same people from before and the same choir and the same offering plate and the same rotting air. Pastor Jim's voice bellows, grating her ears when he talks about sending a bunch of kids to Mexico to save all those poor people—like Mexico's poor people need salvation more than the people staring at him. The kids will go to Mexico and bring the Mexicans to the Lord. And Pastor Jim says when it's time for the offering plate to be sent around, every little bit counts and everyone should give what they can manage. But remember, you can always manage more than you think you can. The organ grinds, rocketing upwards to the Holy Spirit and Pastor Jim is so good, so good he makes tears stream down his cheeks during the final verse of *Go Tell It On the Mountain*. When the song is finished, Pastor Jim's words circle around Harper, spinning and settling in her lap, waiting for her to pick them up and place them onto her tongue and swallow.

'If you baptized in the church, church of Christ, you invited take communion with us, your Holy brethren. Sisters and brothers of our Lord let us take His blood, take His body together at His table.' Harper's mouth is empty, waiting, as conviction is passed around on tin plates. Job snatches a penny-sized wafer and places it on his tongue before immediately shutting his lips. Harper takes the plate from him.

'Wait,' he whispers to her, grabbing a handful of the wafers from the tray, 'I'm starvin.' He thrusts his palm to his mouth.

'Job,' Denise hisses. 'Stop actin like yaint never ate before.

116

This aint no buffet, it's the body of Christ so you best damn act like it.'

He slowly opens his mouth and spits the half-eaten wafers into his hand.

'Now, wait till he tell you to take it,' Denise says.

'Hey,' Job whispers, shoving the handful of wet communion back into his mouth.

'What?'

'This aint real blood.' He brings the cup to his nose and inhales.

'You sure?'

'Not unless Christ bled grape juice.'

Harper bows her head again, feeling the swell of her drunk bloat then condense, back and forth, a pulsing moonshine heart pressing against the inside of her skull as Pastor Jim speaks, his voice bawling in the blessing of the sacrament. Pastor Jim, Jim the reformed sinner, Jim from James, James son of Alpheus, James brother of John, James the apostle, James anointer of tithing allocations, gate keeper of the sin box, James brother in Christ, James brings unholy Mexicans to Christ, James the Holy, Holy by his own accord.

'You asleep?' Job breathes into Harper's ear, his lips almost touching her skin.

'Nah.'

'Why your eyes closed?'

'Tryin to pray.'

'No yaint. When you ever prayed in your life?'

'Shut up—I am too prayin. What do you know anyhow?' Harper says.

'Who you prayin for then?'

'Who you pray for?'

'Well, Mama first. And I pray for you too.'

Harper says nothing.

'Everyone say you need it,' Job says. 'Hey, you wanna hear a joke?'

'Shush now, Job, you hear me?' their daddy says, with dry communion in his hands.

'It's fine, it's bout church.'

'Yeah, gone,' Harper whispers.

'Okay—how you make a nun get rid of her hiccups?'

'Christ Job, quiet.' Denise says without moving her lips.

'How?'

'Tell her she pregnant,' Job says, smiling. 'Nuns can't have babies cause they marry Jesus. You know bout nuns?'

'Yeah,' Harper says.

'How?' Job asks.

'I knew a nun before she got murdered.'

Sixteen, Sixteen and Eighteen

Sister Josephine Paul doesn't look at Harper. Instead, Sister Josephine Paul stirs her coffee, sets the cup down on her desk next to her Bible, sits in the chair behind the desk, opens the Bible to the Gospel of Luke, shuts the Bible, stands up, wipes her glasses clean and paces the length of the room, takes a sip of coffee, adds a bit more sugar, takes another sip of coffee, adds milk, runs her hand over her head. Sister Josephine Paul doesn't wear a habit like normal nuns do. Where her habit should have been, is nothing but a thick pink headband holding her hair back. The pink is bright and pretty against her skin. Sometimes she reminds Harper of Rae Dawn Chong. Or if there is a person mixed between Rae Dawn Chong and Pam Grier. Harper smiles when she thinks about this.

'Would you like to speak to somebody? You could talk to the warden—'

'—the fuck would I tell him?' Harper says, letting her fingernails dig into her palms.

'You can speak to Father—'

'I aint Catholic.' Harper picks at the torn seam of the couch cushion, making the rip longer.

118

Sister Josephine Paul's office is the only room in the entire prison with windows and the windows overlook the yard. Harper stands, walks to the window and peers down. They all stagger in circles, congregating in small groups based on who you hate and who hates you. Daylight casts through the broken blinds and jagged bits of light dance on her desk. Harper sweeps her hand through the light falling onto the Bible.

'I think you should,' Paul says. Her glasses hang around her neck on a thin gold chain. The right pocket of her trousers holds her rosary. Sometimes, she jams her hand into her pocket and rattles the beads, the wood rubbing against itself, calling strength from the Lord. 'She always rattle them beads when I see her,' Tara Hackett had said last week. Paul never rattles the beads around Harper.

'It'll help—it will—'

'She's there cause She sad I'm in here,' Harper says.

'You don't know that.'

Harper says nothing.

'Your Mother's resting now. They'll take good care of Her,' Paul says, wiping her glasses again and returning them to her face.

'Where's *your* mother then?'

'She's at home.'

'She's a good mother, huh?'

'Yes,' Paul says, 'she is.'

'You have a different name before you was a nun—a name your mama gave ya?'

'No.'

'Your mama ever call you Jo?'

'She only called me Jo.'

'—Jo like Jo March?'

'Jo like Jo March.' Sister Paul's shoulders give and she isn't rigid anymore. Her rosary still in her pocket, untouched.

Harper lets her knees give and she settles back into the couch. 'It aint a hospital. Just cause they call it a hospital,

119

don't mean it is one. She might as well be here—She might as well have died face down on the carpet. She aint crazy neither.'

'I know She's not,' Paul says. 'She's resting there so She can't hurt herself anymore, so She can't hurt your brother anymore.'

The backs of Harper's eyelids are tattooed with Job's softly breathing body on the hardwood floor, with Job's face pressed to the soaked mattress, with Job's sobs locked behind the closed door, Job hungry and Job drunk and Job tired. Harper says nothing until she does because it's easy. 'How old are you?'

'Older than you,' Paul says.

'How old's that?'

'Younger than your Mother.'

'She was fourteen you know. How old you been if I was yours?'

'Eleven.'

'How long you been a nun then?'

'Just over a month.'

'That aint very long. I been in here longer than you been a nun.'

'Must be a better prisoner than I am a daughter of the Lord.'

Harper smiles even though Tara Hackett told her not to. Harper laughs even though Tara Hackett told her not to look Sister Paul in the eye. The only thing you do is spit in that nigger's face, Tara Hackett had said.

Harper locks gazes with Paul whose eyes are as handsome as her smile. She has the kind of smile Harper has never seen before, one she thinks she can trust. 'You ever fuck anybody before you was a nun?'

Paul smiles, not showing any of her teeth, and sits on the couch next to Harper. She has the wonderful smell that a book does, or the smell right before it rains. That type of smell that is soft and honest and wonderful and so pure it almost hurts to breathe.

120

'What's his name then?' Harper says.

'Matthew.'

'Was he good?'

'Yes.'

'Meant in bed.'

'Me too,' Paul says.

Harper smiles still, wondering what kind of things you have to do to be a nun who doesn't have to wear a habit and talks to prisoners all day.

'You spend the whole day prayin?'

'No, not the whole day.'

'What you do when you aint prayin?'

'Same thing your Mother does.'

'Yeah? What's that?'

'Wait.'

'Wait for what?' Harper says.

'I wait for God to help me.'

'She aint waitin for nothin. She don't want nothin either and She don't do nothin but sleep.'

'How's that?'

'She's safe when She's sleepin,' Harper says. 'But what if She can't sleep? What if they strap Her down? They gone strap Her down to the bed like a still breathin corpse.'

'I've been there before, visited people there. The doctors do good work,' Paul says.

'They do the Lord's work, huh?'

'I prayed for Her this morning.'

'You the first.' Harper's lies are stale and sour and decaying.

'You're not as good a liar as you think you are.'

Harper scratches at her skin then picks at a scab on her elbow.

'Don't. Stop doing that, it'll scar.' Paul swats at her hand. 'I pray for you too, you know.'

'You pray for Tara Hackett?'

Paul takes her hand from the coffee cup and places it in her right pocket. It doesn't move but Harper hears the sound of wood rubbing wood. 'All the time.'

'She hates you.'

'Why?'

'Cause you know Jesus and cause you nice and cause she a bigot. She wants you dead cause you called me in here and she wants you dead cause you pray for me.'

Paul says nothing.

'But I'm glad you do.'

'Why?'

'I dunno yet,' Harper says, the truth dripping from her tongue. 'Don't worry about that other shit—Tara Hackett hates most people.'

'She doesn't hate you though, does she?'

'She chose me.'

'Why you?'

'I dunno.'

'Well, maybe then you chose her.'

'I aint like that—I aint like her—but when I got here I couldn't stop shiverin and sweatin at the same time and she said she liked how I talk and the things I said but I aint like that—I'm just—' Harper's tongue stills and words slip back into her belly. 'Tara Hackett hates you. Why you pray for someone who hates you? What do you say when you pray for Tara Hackett? What'd you ask God for?'

'I pray she'll forgive herself for what she's done and that God will let her see her children again.'

'She'd hate you even more if she knew that.'

Sister Paul says nothing.

'I won't say nothing,' Harper says.

Sister Paul paces to the window and pulling the cord, the blind opens further so that sunlight floods the room.

'You need to pray for Job.' Harper blinks in the light.

'Why?'

'Don't no one hear my prayers.'

Every day after that day, I went to her office or she'd call for me to give me a book from the library or help with my equivalency tests. And she always smiled at me and told me I was different and special even though she didn't understand why I done what I done. She said I was a blessing and that one day, Caro and Collier would know that what I did was for all of us. And she always held my hand and maybe the only thing God ever done for me was give me Sister Josephine Paul.

Nineteen, Nineteen and Twenty-One

The congregation spills from the sanctuary onto the lawn and into the street. With their arms linked, Tillie and Caro make their way to Harper.

'How are you, Luke?' Tillie says.

He leans in and kisses her cheek, then does the same to Caro.

'Mr Haley, Miss Denise.' Caro's gaze sinks to the ground. Her face is bloated and greasy with exhaustion and last night's drunk.

'Tillie, Carolyn.' Denise crosses her arms.

'Afternoon now, Job.' Tillie smoothes his hair and kisses him on the forehead. He leans into her touch then stills.

'Hi.' Harper's daddy pinches Job's side. 'Afternoon, Mrs Naylor.'

'Afternoon, Harper.' Tillie takes Harper's right hand and pulls her in. 'You come round again real soon,' she says, slipping a ten-dollar bill into Harper's palm. 'But don't you ever wear that dress again. You go home and either hang it back up where it belong or you burn it. You hear me?'

'You look like shit,' Harper whispers to Caro.

'Yall both do,' Tillie mumbles, threading her frail wing into Caro's arm as they walk from the steeple. 'Look and smell like sin. Both yall look like damn trash.'

Harper's daddy jams his hand into his pocket and rattles the car keys. The stiff collar of his shirt falls limp in the heat. Job wipes his face with his tie leaving the navy fabric damp with sweat.

'You need a cut. It's gettin a bit long.' Harper's daddy runs his hand through Job's hair then thumbs the scar at this temple.

'No it aint.'

He smiles at his son and kisses him on top of his head. 'Yall wait here, I'll bring the car round.'

The traffic light blinks yellow to red and the car slows to a stop.

'Job, you can get outside to mow the lawn after lunch, all right? Got three dollars if you do a good job,' Harper's daddy says, rolling down his window, letting the heat breathe into the car.

'It's Sunday.'

'I used to mow on Sundays.'

Job laughs. 'Whatcha doin mowin your daddy's yard anyhow? Thought he had niggers for that.'

Harper's daddy spins so fast she feels a breeze on her face. Revving back he pops Job straight in the mouth. And she'll never forget the sound of her father's knuckles on Job's pink little boy skin. Harper figures he hit him because Job can still be saved and that Job is still worth saving. Harper's skin doesn't sting but she wishes it did.

Job doesn't cry or blink or do anything, just sits there like a little stunned statue.

'Don't you ever,' Harper's daddy begins, 'hey, you goddam look at me boy—don't you ever run your mouth like that to me or nobody else. Ya hear me?'

'Yessir.'

'Running your mouth like you better'd other people. Didn't raise my kid to talk like some piece a trash. Ya hear me son?'

'Yessir.'

Harper's daddy gives Job a fat lip, split down the middle

with blood collecting at the bottom of his chin. Harper tries to dab it with the hem of Her dress but he jerks away.

'Take you down to French Camp so you can mow lawns and get the shit knocked outta you. Give you somethin to complain about then. How bout that?'

'Filthy fuckin niggers,' Harper whispers, knowing that he'll hear her.

Without hesitation he turns around again and this time boxes Job in his right ear, forcing his head into the window. 'You testin me boy?' He draws back again and gives him a clean smack across his still bleeding face.

Job says nothing. Just cowers into the window and shuts his eyes with his face looking damp. 'No, sir.'

'No, sir what?'

'No, sir, aint testin you.'

'Say it again boy. Keep talkin that filth—I dare you boy. I dare you to keep talkin filthy shit like that.'

With his eyes still closed, Job wipes away snot and hushed tears with the back of his hand. Harper aches and her stomach creeps up above her lungs into her throat. She watches Job and prays. Prays that he'll never forget what that hand felt like when he says something horrible. With her eyes open, Harper prays that God will save Job. Harper prays that God will have mercy on Job, prays that God will spare him.

I pray for you more than any person I have ever known or loved.

Nineteen, Nineteen and Twenty-One
Sitting in the kitchen with the radio turned down real low, Harper refills her glass three times and hides the empty bottle behind the refrigerator after an hour of spinning through dead air and advertisements for call-in medicine. It's after three in the morning when she's pressing her fifth cigarette into the

125

countertop and the phone rings. The shrill loop stops when she pulls the receiver from the wall.

Collier's voice is quietly breathless. '—Exxon towards Caro's.'

The only working streetlight of the four shines and flickers on Tommy's truck and burnt out tire tracks. There are two busted gas pumps and an air hose with a cracked nozzle sprawling out like an abandoned snakeskin on the gasoline-soaked concrete. Tommy's truck is parked next to a deserted white van with three tires and a mud spattered windshield.

Tommy stands on the pavement. He's kicking at the door and screaming his voice hoarse. Picking up an empty gas jug, he throws it into the windshield before tripping over his own feet and falling into the hood of the truck.

'You stupid faggot—' Collier yells through the passenger's window. Sitting in the front seat, she waves her middle finger at him and nurses a long swig from a full bottle.

He struggles to stand. Dancing in a puddle of unleaded gas and shards of broken beer bottles, his boots crunch out a beat like a metronome. Thick green veins bulge in his arms and neck and face. 'Get out, you piece a shit.' He kicks at the bumper, loses his balance again and falls to the ground.

Harper runs past him, sliding along the fender to the passenger side door. Collier pushes it open and pulls Harper's body to her own. Snot and saliva coat Collier's face—thick black tracks of mascara smudge down to the tops of her cheekbones. She leans across Harper and locks the door. Turning the keys in the ignition, the engine revs. Collier punches the gas with the gearshift still in park. There's a swift crack and a dent bulges in her side window.

'Where he get a brick?'

Tommy knocks through the plexiglass, his arms springing through her window. Grabbing her by the neck, blood runs down his forearms as he drives Collier's head into the steering wheel.

'Don't look at him,' Collier says with his fingers rigid and clamped around her throat. 'Don't look at him.' Harper tries prying his hands loose and she inhales his breath. His smell fills the car—his scent of burning wood and acid and chemicals and piss and expired snuff, smelling like a carcass left in the sun. He has a shine on his arms and hands that isn't sweat. His limbs are smeared with ash, and he rots still.

'Can't be full blown dyke when you cock ride so much can you, Collier?'

Collier bucks back and he loses his grip on her. She kicks her door open and his knees give. Grabbing at his stomach, he lays on the ground, screaming and carrying on and calling her the names he always has. Harper says nothing, she just watches Collier watching Tommy rolling around on the pavement blind drunk. Collier's panting, leaning back into her headrest, she closes her eyes, but it's Caro that's the one who's always been good at praying.

Harper grabs the crowbar sitting at Collier's feet then unlocks her door. Walking next to the tailgate she notices a crumpled baseball jersey in its bed. He's still yelling but hasn't found the will or way to stand. Harper picks up the dirt and gasoline-stained white jersey and sees Tommy's name, his daddy's name, stitched across the shoulders above a crimson number seven. Burkett. She takes the lighter from her pocket, flicks it to life and shoves it into the fabric. She tosses it on the ground next to him after it catches.

'Christ you doing, you bitch?'

She's holding the crowbar in a loose grip. Her wrist bounces easily, finding its rhythm in her breaths and blinks. Her heartbeat stutters in her throat, between her legs, behind her kneecaps. Rust flakes scrape against her palm and she's drunk on knowing that Collier can take a punch just as good as she gives. Because when Harper was six and Collier was eight and Tommy was ten, he tried teaching them how to scrap. 'Gotta know how to protect yall self,' he had said.

Harper sat on the bed of Tommy's daddy's truck and watched Tommy and Collier, both topless in the heat, box in his daddy's driveway. Tommy had squeezed and punched at Collier's soft flesh, his knuckles catching the planks of her girl-but-not-yet-girl body. He left scrapes, bruises and cuts to show her, to show everybody, where he'd been, to leave his mark on her. Harper had watched Tommy push Collier to the ground, straddle her, humping her in-between girl body and smacking her across the face over and over. All before holding his forearm against her windpipe. Harper just sat there and Collier wheezed. He laughed as he took one of her nipples between his fingers with a hard pinch. But then Harper saw Tommy tumble as Collier drove her clenched fist into his left side. Collier took some of him with her, his skin and blood under her fingernails as she cut deep scratches all over him. Harper had smiled while Tommy whimpered, lying on his left side while Collier stood up and stomped down into his ribs, scratched at his eyes and spit in his face. When Collier gave him a final punch to the gut, his body convulsed in silent weeping. He had never told anyone about that day. Collier had never told anyone. Harper had never told anyone. But thinking about that day now, Harper knows Tommy has never been able to hide his left side.

Harper walks to him, raises the crowbar above her head like she's about to chop wood and brings it down into his left side.

He screams and gropes at his ribs. His eyes are shut and he's wincing, lying on his back with his legs outstretched. 'You uh, you aint change a bit, huh? Only thing yall cunts like more than gettin it, is beggin for it.' A sluggish smile spreads across his face.

Harper steps over him, straddling him. She raises the crowbar again and brings it down clean into his jaw. Then again. Then again. Then his shoulder. Then a few more times. He's bleeding black now. Then again. His body is spilling oil, leaking black

gold. If there could be something more than bleeding—
something thicker and heavier, some type of oozing and exodus
that brings you closer to death than blood can—this is it. Then
again. Then a few more times. Sometimes, corpses aren't dead.
Sometimes, corpses aint never dead.

'Stop,' Collier breathes into Harper's ear, gently pulling her
back by her elbows towards the truck. 'Ya gotta—ya gotta
stop. Don't—they'll send you back.' Collier wipes his blood
the best she can from Harper's hands onto her own. 'Cmon,
we gotta—we uh, cmon.'

As Collier drives she doesn't look like herself. She's nothing.
She's nothing but a cicada shell of the girl she is in daylight
and her pupils have been replaced with small, black bruises.

'You shouldn't be drivin like this.'

'This is it. Last time. It is, honest,' Collier mumbles to herself,
her eyes on the road, unblinking. She flicks her tongue against
her bottom lip like a drunken serpent, tasting the blood Tommy's
knuckles had drawn. 'Don't tell Her.'

'What?'

'If you ever see your Mama again, please don't tell Her I let
this happen.'

Twelve, Twelve and Fourteen

'Yall get in here,' She says, leaning against the doorframe, a
spoon hanging from Her mouth.

'It aint even dark yet.' Harper bounces a tennis ball to Caro
who catches and returns it. Collier sits in the driveway, her
knees pulled to her chest, picking at her nail polish and staring
at the ground.

'I didn't ask what time it is. Caro, Collier cmon, yall too.'

Caro and Collier echo 'Yes, M'am' in unison and climb the
stairs to the front door.

Tommy's oversized camouflage shorts pull at his hips, bare-chested, the lean planks of his muscles defined and cut, a boy with a body like brick that'll never bruise.

'Get goin, Tommy.'

He laughs, stepping onto the porch and stands eye to eye with Her. 'My daddy loves gettin called here.'

'Your daddy can suck his own dick all the way to hell—get goin and stop botherin my girls all the time.'

'Aint no little girls.' He smiles pretty and brushes a lock of hair behind Her ear. 'Only thing they love more than gettin it, is beggin for it.'

She spits into his face before the sole of Her foot meets his stomach and they watch him collapse next to the driveway, his ass breaking his fall, yelling the words his daddy taught him. She jumps, clearing the steps and lands next to him, a brick in Her right hand, the spoon in Her left. Spitting again into his face, the brick meets his jaw in a broken kiss.

'Go cry to your daddy, cocksucker,' She whispers, letting the brick collide with his bleeding smile until Harper pulls Her away, strips the brick from Her hand and then spits on Tommy herself.

'How many times I tell yall the same damn things? How many?' She shouts, flicking the deadbolt forward and then pulling the blinds shut. 'I'm tired sayin the same damn things over and over cause yall wanna act nasty all the time.' She drops the spoon into an uncapped jar of crunchy peanut butter and takes a long slug from Her tumbler. 'How many—how many damn times I say don't bring him round? That sorry asshole don't have a chance in hell—he'll be his daddy soon enough then yall will listen to me but it'll be too late. Just wait—'

The television blares. Two women screech with laughter and order Wild Turkey, Coke, a shot of Jose Cuervo and a Margarita.

'Where's Job?' Harper asks, sifting through a month old stack of unopened mail.

'You his Mama now or somethin?' She fingers a cigarette and flicks a Zippo, taking long drags and letting Her eyelids flutter underneath the breath of the ceiling fan.

'Whatcha watchin, Luce?' Caro laps at the spoonful of peanut butter, gripping the handle where Her fingers have just been.

'Movie.'

Collier shakes a cigarette from the pack on the table and She swipes them from her hand. 'What are you doing? You gone ask?'

'Since when I gotta ask?'

'You ask today,' She says with heavy breath and brick grated palms.

'Why?'

'Scuse me?'

'Can I get a cigarette?'

'What's that?'

'Can I get a cigarette, M'am?' Collier looks to the floor while chewing her tongue.

'You gone bring that piece of shit Tommy Burkett round here again?'

'No, M'am.'

'You gone stop actin like a stray?'

'Yes, M'am.'

'Help yourself.'

'Can we watch?'

'Sure ya can, Caro—you the good one, you know that?' She falls into the couch, the glass spitting drink over its lip. 'Yall two hear that? Caro's the good one.'

Collier lights the cigarette then hands it to Harper who takes a drag then exhales towards her Mother.

'Good for you, girl.' She smiles with her mouth wet and her eyes glowing. 'You lucky you look like your Mama when you suck on a cigarette.'

'My mama don't like films with swearin,' Caro says. She holds the jar of peanut butter with hands covered in mosquito

131

bites, swollen welts she can't help but scratch even though Tillie says not to.

'Shut the fuck up, Caro,' Collier says, peeking through the blinds.

'Knock it off, Collier—Caro that's cause your mama likes beautiful words and she sounds beautiful when she talks to God. You best pray you turn out like her.'

'I do.'

'Good girl—yall two listen to Caro. Yall shouldn't be swearin, it makes yall both sound like real trash.'

Harland's shirt is tucked into his jeans and his sleeves are cuffed at his biceps. A lock of blond hair falls forward and all he does is grin, leaning over Thelma and asking her to dance.

'That's how shit always starts—nothin good ever comes from a drink and a smile from a stranger.'

Harper watches Her float between yesterday's high and the morning's exhaustion. Cotton-mouthed with puffy eyes, a foul sneer, She reclines on the couch next to Caro and exhales a dark breath towards the ceiling. 'Whatcha lookin at, girl?'

'Where's Job?'

'Come sit and watch. Cmon. He's fine, he's sleepin.'

Harper stalks into the hallway and opens Job's door. The small, windowless room reeks of piss and vomit. Job is lying facedown in his paint-chipped crib, naked and asleep and silent. The right side of his face presses against the soiled and soaked mattress. She places her hand on his back, feeling the faint breaths of his body. She pulls the pacifier from his mouth and smells the rubber before placing it into her own. She tongues the nipple, tasting Her, sticky and sour. Chewing the pacifier in a slow grind, she softly pinches Job's nose shut. His eyelids flutter but do not open. And he does not stir. She wishes she was brave but all she does is stand there, palming Job's skull and begging God to save him.

Harland's hands paw at Thelma's skin in drunken gropes, fumbling at the buttons of her dress. With three slaps, Harland forces her down on the car hood, bends her over so her body is pressed flat, ass in the air. Bleeding from her nostrils, her feet slip on the oil slick pavement. He pushes her dress up to her shoulder blades. Drool rains from Harland's mouth and falls onto her bare back.

Louise presses the barrel to the fleshy spot beneath his earlobe and behind his jaw.

'Shit, she gone kill him,' Caro yells, her eyes locked on Susan Sarandon's face and the gun steady in her hands.

'You watch, Caro. Sometimes it only takes one shot, but sometimes more.'

With his fly open and belt hanging limp from his hip, he slumps against the fender. A crimson flower blooms against his white shirt. Louise's hands are shaking. Her eyes are wide. Her mouth hangs slack.

'Only took one.' Caro sucks on the spoon again. 'I woulda shot him twice.'

'Yall listen to Caro—she's the smart one. And you don't forget Louise and what she done cause she had to.'

Harper watches the three of them on the couch, shoulder to shoulder and scowling at the television screen, with their legs pulled to their chests. Their faces are thin, scarred and tired. Collier and Luce swap drags of Her cigarette while Caro rests against Her side then closes her eyes when She gently grazes Her fingernails through hair that shines in the same beautiful shade as Tillie's. Collier lays her empty hand on Luce's knee.

133

Luce squeezes the back of Collier's neck in slow beats. Sitting between them, touching them, She sinks down into the couch, settling and still and quiet.

Collier turns to her. 'Didn't even know you left.'

And Harper says nothing.

'Harper—'

'Yes, M'am?'

'You walk over there and rewind the tape and watch Louise's hands till it's the only goddam thing you see at night when you close your eyes,' She says.

Nineteen, Nineteen and Twenty-One

They leave Tommy's truck parked but still running in an empty creek bed off Route 3 and then walk in silence to Caro's house. Lightning bugs tread at their noses and Harper catches one but quickly releases it. She says nothing when it trails off into the darkness. The air cools and in the dark there is a freshness, a breath from daytime swelter.

'You do it.' Collier faces the road with her back to Harper as they stand on Caro's porch. 'Please—you do it.'

Harper knocks on the door gently, hoping Caro will hear but Tillie won't. The porch light flickers on and off as moths swarm the dying light bulb. Caro opens the door and through the screen Harper watches her rub the sleep from her eyes. They widen when Caro sees Harper's hands and Collier's face.

'What happened?' she says, yanking them into the house. 'What's wrong?'

'Just for the night,' Collier says.

'Yeah, sure. Come on.'

Collier tosses her purse onto the couch and it falls open. Caro pulls a filthy plastic bag of weed from it.

'When are you going to stop holding for Tommy?'

'It's for your mama,' Collier says.

Caro holds the bag tight. 'Thank you.'

Collier says nothing.

'Thank you, Collier.'

'I heard you.'

'You should change, go get something in the back, Collier,' Caro says. 'Jesus, look at your hands—'

Harper's hands are stained with blood, drips of Tommy's drunken unclotted life and black tarnish.

'We need to wash them.'

They stand shoulder to shoulder at the sink. Harper turns away from the mirror. Caro tests the temperature of the running water with her own fingers and opens the cold spigot further, then scrubs a bar of soap across Harper's knuckles. Her skin burns but not enough to say anything. It hurts so she figures it's good for her. Pink foam spills and funnels down the drain.

'Yall been drinking?'

'Not me.'

'You smell cheap,' Caro says. She massages Harper's hands with the soap. 'I feel drunk when you breathe on me. You smell like sin.'

Harper smiles at Tillie's words.

'All Denise buy is cheap cause she a cheap hooker,' Harper says. 'And I can't sleep.'

'Stop making fists. It won't hurt as much if you stop making fists.'

Harper loosens her hands while Caro rinses them, picking small bits of rust from her palms.

'Where is he?'

'I dunno, still layin on the cement over at the Exxon I guess.'

'Jesus Christ, Harper.'

'They been drinkin I think.'

'What happened?'

'Dunno,' Harper says. 'She didn't say nothin on the way here.'

'What happened?'

Harper says nothing.

'Nothing's ever going to change. Look at you, wishing, thinking it will. Nothing is going to change here. Never,' Caro says. Harper says nothing and Caro surrenders. 'What happened when you were done with him?'

'I won't never be done with him.'

'You hurt him?'

'Yeah, I think so.'

'Good,' Caro says, closing the taps. She dries Harper's hands with a towel and turns off the bathroom light. 'You can sleep in my bed. More blankets in the closet if you need them.'

'It's too hot.'

'I'll be back in a minute.'

'Where you goin?'

'I said I'll be back in a minute.'

Harper collapses into the unmade sheets and she never hears or feels Caro come into bed.

'Whatcha creepin round for? You hungry?' Tillie sits rocking in her chair, taking long puffs on a cigarette and fingering the spine of her Bible.

'No thank you, m'am.' Harper stands in the doorway, watching Tillie.

'I said—you hungry?'

'Sort of,' Harper says, 'a bit, I guess.'

Tillie stubs the cigarette into an ashtray and hacks violently, shaking her head. 'Caro, you gone be late if you don't move,' she calls into the back while leading Harper into the kitchen.

'I said I'm coming,' Caro yells.

'Morning.' Collier walks into the kitchen, kisses Tillie on the cheek and then sits at the table.

'Morning, Collier.' Tillie lights the stove and a small blue flame ignites after three clicks. 'Yaint been round in a while. Nice to see you.'

'You too, m'am.'

Caro rushes into the kitchen with an unzipped backpack hanging from her shoulder, three textbooks and a notebook nearly spilling out. She grabs an apple from the counter and shoves it into her bag.

'Look here,' Tillie says, smiling and handing Collier a tissue to wipe her face, 'been a real long time since I been in the same room with all my pretty ones.'

Thirteen, Thirteen and Fifteen

'Christ Caro, open a window. Hot as hell,' Collier says. With one hand she swats at Caro who's fiddling with the small stereo, and with the other she holds a bottle of dark nail polish. A cigarette hangs from her lips, ash falls onto her bare thighs. 'And change station while you at it.'

'Why?'

'Cause I don't like him.'

'Why?' Harper says.

'Cause I don't. You know he aint even black no more.'

'Oh sure he is,' Caro says.

'No he aint—he got his face bleached and his songs are shit. Here, put this in.' Collier hands Caro an unmarked cassette tape.

Caro rolls her eyes and jams the tape into the stereo, rewinds it, pushes Play. Collier mumbles the lyrics of the song under her breath like the words are her own.

'Why ya want black, Harper?' Caro says, falling into her bed.

'I like black nails,' Harper says as Collier drags the brush dripping with dark polish from the cuticle to the tip of her nail. Collier is precise and has a real steady hand.

Caro's arms hang over the edge of her bed as she flicks through the newspaper lying on the floor. Bush's front-page face is fading with Tillie's fingerprints. 'Are yalls daddies Republicans?'

'Ask Harper—she the only who knows,' Collier says. 'But they all is.'

'All Republicans what?'

'Daddies,' Collier says, exhaling a breath of smoke out the corner of her mouth. 'All daddies are Republicans. Cmon Caro, you next. Whatcha want? Ya want pink? You look like a girl who loves pretty pink nails and pretty pink boys with pretty pink skin.'

'Nah. I want black too.'

'Good, black all we got.'

'You look like Lauren Hutton when you paint nails, except yaint got buck teeth,' Caro says.

'Yeah, Lauren Hutton, but Lauren Hutton mixed with someone else,' Harper says.

'Lauren Hutton and who?' A row of ash falls from Collier's lips to the carpet.

'I know—you look like if Lauren Hutton and Julie Christie could have a baby. That's what you look like,' Harper says, as Collier pauses to take the cigarette from her own mouth and place it between Harper's lips.

'Who's that?'

'Oh you know,' Caro says, 'she like British or Franch or somethin.'

'She's in *Shampoo*.'

'My mama don't let me watch that trash.'

'It aint trash,' Collier says.

'She sleep with Warren Beatty and she's in *Heaven Can Wait*,' Harper says.

'Her hair looks terrible. Collier, you said it was my turn.'

'No, I said you next.' Collier blows on the fingernails of Harper's right hand. She dips the brush back into the paint and then pulls Harper's left hand towards her.

'Yeah her hair looks terrible but her face don't. She's got a great face.'

138

'She got good tits?'

'Yeah,' Harper and Caro say in unison.

Collier smiles real big.

'Lovechild a Julie Christie and Lauren Hutton, that's good. Do me now,' Caro says.

'Hmmm Carolyn Naylor,' Collier begins.

'Stop callin me at all the time.' Caro throws a pen at Collier that falls short.

'Well, you half Diane Lane—'

'Gross.'

'What? Diane Lane's pretty,' Harper says.

'She's weird lookin.'

'You ever seen a real picture of her?'

'No but—' Caro begins.

'Go look in the mirror then, she'll be staring right back at you. So half Diane Lane—'

'—half Debra Winger,' Harper says.

'*Urban Cowboy* or *Officer*?'

'*Cowboy*,' Caro shoves the newspaper under her bed.

'You can't just pick,' Collier says.

'Sure I can, I made this up. Won't for me, we wouldn't be playin.'

'Me too, I think *Cowboy*,' Harper says.

'Fine. Now you.' Collier leans down, blowing real soft on Harper's fingertips again. 'Whatcha think, Caro?'

'A little Jackie O maybe?'

'Yeah, a little,' Collier says, 'but you gotta mix all that smile with someone who has a face with lines on it.'

'I aint got no wrinkles.'

'Wrinkles aint the same as lines. Lines are different. Lines, you know, like on your Mama's face. Jackie O's a good start though. She's a bit soft lookin, that's why you need somebody with lines. People that got lines seen real shit. Maybe like—like Jackie O and Anne Bancroft.'

'Yeah?'

'Yeah, that's all right,' Caro says. 'That's a good one.'

'Anne Bancroft's got a face a sharp lines and she's got real nice tits too,' Collier says. 'Cmon, your turn, Caro.'

Caro and Harper switch spots. The bed is warm from Caro's body. They barely hear the phone ring over the sixth rotation of *Cooky Puss*. Under Caro's closed door, Tillie's feet shuffle from the kitchen to her bedroom, back to the kitchen, to the bathroom, back to the kitchen and then to Caro's room. She taps gently on the door three times before it creeps open with Tillie's small body standing in the frame.

'—yall doin?' Tillie says. 'Jesus, the hell's wrong with you, Ann-Collier, smokin in my house like that?' Tillie plucks the cigarette from Collier's lips and places it between her own. She takes a long drag and exhales towards Harper. 'Don't yall be doin this. It'll make you real sick.'

'You'll get sick too,' Collier says.

'Already am, smartass. Sides, I'm trying to save yall best I can.' Tillie winks at Harper. 'And seems I'm out of cough syrup, again. Now I got a tickle in my throat but got to go spend more money on more Robitussin. Why's that, Caro? When we just had a full bottle a day ago?'

Caro just looks at Collier who the day before had told them to be real careful because if they drank all of it, like Collier told them to do, and wasn't careful about it like Collier said to be, they'd just go and puke it all up. Then everything would be a waste. Collier and Caro look at the floor but Harper's eyes stray up.

'Shouldn't look at me, Miss,' Tillie says, 'you know about my missin things?'

'No, m'am.'

'Well, if it turn up, let me know. But look here, I'm runnin out for a minute, yall need anythin? Yall be okay for a minute?'

'Where you going?' Caro asks.

'Just runnin out.'

'Where you goin?' Harper says.

'I'm seein your Mama real quick.'

They say nothing.

'She's fine, just gone help Her get sorted real quick before your daddy get home. Just take a minute—She got an appointment I'm helping Her with.'

Harper says nothing as Her secret and Her words from that night when they walked in the street climb up her throat and spin in her ear.

Tillie presses her lips to her ear. 'It's for the best, sweetheart. It is.'

'Can I come with you?' Harper asks. They let it be quiet and Tillie takes the cigarette from her mouth and kisses Harper.

'Stay here, let your nails dry.' Tillie grabs Harper's hand, looking close at the clean detail around the cuticle. 'Real nice job, Collier.'

'Don't I know it,' she says not looking up from Caro's nails.

Tillie takes a final pull and returns the cigarette to Collier's mouth. 'This last time I'm tellin you, no smokin in my house. You don't smoke in here no more, Ann-Collier. This the last one.'

'Yes, m'am.'

'Stay here,' Tillie whispers to Harper. 'Keep them out of trouble for me.'

'Yes, m'am.'

'Everythin's fine. She'll be fine. It's for the best. Yall be good, I mean it.' Tillie shuts the door behind her. 'And stay outta my cabinets.'

'Hey,' Collier calls, 'Hey, Harper—'

Caro's right. Collier looks an awful lot like Lauren Hutton. Caro's nails are only half done but she rolls next to Harper in bed, scooting real close to her, the edges of their bodies touching. Collier sits at the foot of the bed, leaning against the wall propping herself up on her elbows.

'She'll be fine,' Collier says real quiet. 'Ya know Caro, Tillie look like Meryl Streep if Meryl Streep had dark hair.'

'*Deer Hunter* or *Kramer vs. Kramer*?' Caro says, shoving her body even closer to Harper.

'She look the same in both,' Collier says.

'No she don't.'

'Yeah she do.'

'Well, more like *Deer Hunter*,' Caro says, 'I guess.'

'Yeah.' Collier caps the nail polish. 'I can see that.'

Nineteen, Nineteen and Twenty-One

'Breakfast?' Tillie asks, lighting another cigarette.

'Nah, I have to get to work. I'm late as it is,' Caro says.

'You got somethin for lunch then?'

'Yeah, I'm fine. And put that out, you're making it worse.'

'What time you home, Caro?'

'Eight, maybe nine. I'll call.' Caro kisses her mother on the cheek then with her lips pressed to Tillie's ear, she whispers, 'Love you.'

'Love you too,' Tillie says real quiet.

Harper and Collier stand in the kitchen silent and just taking up space, watching Tillie and Caro. Caro kisses Harper, then Collier and squeezes her hand.

'Thank you,' Caro says to Collier. 'Bye.'

'How yall want your eggs?' Tillie asks while she flicks ash into a dirty mug.

Collier shrugs. Her face is still filthy and her greasy hair is pulled back, exposing a large bruise on the left side of her forehead. A long pink and brown scab on her right ear is ripped open, leaking pus.

'I said how yall want your eggs, Harper?'

'How you have them?'

'I like scrambled eggs, you know that.' Tillie cracks an egg against a ceramic bowl.

'Scrambled please, m'am,' Harper says sitting at the table.

'Collier?'

142

'Scrambled please, m'am.'

Tillie cooks and fries until the shelves of her refrigerator are barren. She serves them each a large plate and Collier barely breathes between mouthfuls.

'Christ Almighty, girl, it aint gone run from ya.' Tillie joins them at the table. She's drinking black coffee, its grains sprinkled around the rim of the chipped cup. 'Caro didn't tell me yall comin round last night.'

Collier says nothing.

'Just droppin by,' Harper says, saving her.

'Dropping by four in the mornin, huh?' Tillie's eggs sit untouched on her plate. She takes long sips of coffee followed by long drags from her cigarette.

'Figured that—' Collier begins with a mouth full of food.

'Just that—we knew she had work but didn't know when she finish—'

'Yall in trouble?' Tillie asks.

'No, m'am,' Harper says.

'Collier, I said yall in trouble?'

'No, m'am. No trouble for nobody.' She looks into her plate.

'What good things happen four in the mornin?'

'I'm sorry, Tillie,' Harper says.

'No trouble for me, aint nothin I won't sleep through but yall know that. Now, Collier?'

'Yes, m'am?'

'Wanna tell me where Tommy's at?'

'Dunno where he's at, m'am.'

'Aint never seen you so quiet, Ann-Collier.'

'I'm real tired.'

'Tommy causin you trouble?'

'No, m'am.' Collier isn't half the liar Harper is.

'Janet Marshall been sayin for months there's awful lot of comin and goin round his daddy's cabin. Yall wouldn't know nothin bout that, now would you?'

'No, m'am,' they say in unison.

'Crank'll kill you, you know that Collier? You hear me?'

'Yes, m'am.'

'You got anythin to add to all this?'

'No, m'am,' Harper says.

'I don't do nothin like that, Tillie,' Collier says. 'I aint like that.'

'I know you don't. Both yall smart girls when you wanna be, when the mood strike ya right. Now Collier, Tommy been cookin in Bart's cabin?'

'No, m'am.'

Tillie takes another drag and slides her plate across the table. 'You still got yourself an awful pretty smile, Ann-Collier.'

Collier stares into the plate of food, unable to look at Tillie or Harper.

'When you this quiet, Ann-Collier, it's like you already dead.' Tillie sucks on her cigarette in long breaths. 'Well, yall come and get me when you're done lyin. Can't force yall to do nothin—learned that a long time ago.'

Collier finishes her plate in heaping spoonfuls. Tillie takes her in slowly before reaching out with her empty hand to push Collier's blinding hair behind her ear. She tries to suppress a flinch but can't when Tillie's bony hand gently grazes the bruise.

'Thank you,' Harper says.

'For what? Yaint eat nothin, and Collier—'

'Yes, m'am?' Collier stands with her hands in her back pockets, her posture perfect, her tits pushed out proud like last night hadn't even happened.

'Why don't you go and have a wash? Then after you can have a rest for a bit.'

Tillie leaves then quickly returns with a pile of Caro's clothes and a towel. Collier says nothing.

'Cmon, don't got all day now, girl. And Collier, stay out of my medicine cabinet. You go in that cabinet and you leavin.'

Collier forces a smile and nods. The only person who has

ever bothered to tell Collier not to do something is Tillie. With her lips pressed together in a straight line, Collier walks to the end of the hall then shuts the bathroom door behind her.

Harper and Tillie stand together and keep standing when they hear Collier's voice crack, her sobbing muffled by the running jet of the shower.

I don't know what day of the week it was that Collier died but I know it was June, five summers later. It was summer, it always was.

She was cold to the touch when Tillie found her—that's what Caro said. And there was a bruise at the base of her throat and you couldn't even tell she was four months gone when Tillie opened the bathroom door and saw Collier's corpse hugging her knees next to the toilet bowl. Caro said Tillie wiped the vomit from her mouth and shut her eyelids before she knelt and prayed for her. Caro told me she asked Tillie why she prayed, because there wasn't a reason to, not a single one. Then Tillie told her if they had been in the same room instead of talking on the phone that she would have slapped the shit out of her for saying something so nasty, for speaking so crude of her sister. And that made Caro hate Collier even more.

Collier thought she was saving the little girl inside her so they went quietly, in silence, into the sleep that Collier had chosen. That's what I tell myself. And I tell myself that last handful pills she'd swiped from Tillie made her feel good and warm and gave her peace. Maybe Collier thought she was doing them both a favour, saving both of them, but I don't know because nobody know what Collier thought. Never. People always tried to change Collier—save her and baptize her into a lady. But she was fine with the girl she made herself to be. She was proud of who she was and I think that's what scared people the most—that she chose what she was. But Collier is the one nobody remembers and that's why her voice will never still.

It happened because we weren't there. We left her, did the only thing she couldn't bear. So she went and did it to herself. By herself. After everything that had happened and everything that was, it was me and Caro that broke her. We took that oath, the three of us, and when we did, Collier swore that if me and Caro ever left her, she'd kill herself. And when Caro graduated school and Denise finally found the courage to snitch on me to Bart, Collier kept her word.

Me and Caro are the only ones who remember Collier but it's for the best.

Nineteen, Nineteen and Twenty-One
Tillie grabs Harper's hand. 'You got shit circulation cause of drink and tobacco.'

'Nah.'

'Cold hands, warm heart, that's what you got. Let's go on the porch.'

'I wanna wait for Collier.'

'Let her rest a bit, she be all right. She'll learn be all right without ya. Just gotta let her. Let her learn on her own. Come on outside, it's real pretty today.'

'It's hot.'

'It's always hot.' Tillie eases into the white wicker chair with cheap paint peeling off its frame. Harper sits on the first splintered step of the porch. Tillie opens the bag Collier brought her and begins to roll a joint.

'When's the last time you slept?'

'This mornin.' Harper stares straight into the sun, pressing her thumb into a rusted nailhead.

'The bags you got under your eyes is old. You got rotten, lost sleep hangin from your eyes. You look hollow in a way you never been. Your Mama be on Her deathbed seein you like this. You clean?'

'Yeah.'

146

'You lyin to me? Yall need stop carryin on like this all the time. You can't get and stay like this all day every day.'

'I don't get anythin—I just am.'

'Well, you can thank your Mama for that.'

'I'm tired. I wish I wasn't. I can't sleep unless I'm here.'

'Why's that?'

'Get nightmares sometimes,' Harper says, not knowing why she's saying things that are true. 'I dunno—just tired.'

'Nightmares about what?'

'Just that, it's real quiet at night. That don't help.'

'Thought you might want some quiet.'

'Me too,' Harper says.

'Things just changin is all, keep your eyes above the water, girl.' Tillie licks the joint's edge. 'You'll fall back into it.'

'Yeah? When?'

'You will. Couldn't sleep for a year after Caro's sister passed. I was so angry at God I couldn't breathe.'

Harper has never heard Tillie say Olivia's name, never heard Tillie talk about Dennis after he left, after Olivia was born dead. Caro spoke about Olivia only once, when they were nine and nine and eleven. Caro said the whole thing made her so sad because she always wanted a little sister and she had been asking God for one for a real long time. So how come He made her little sister come out of her mama already dead? Why did God finally give her one just to take her away? Collier told Caro not to worry—that this kind of thing happened a lot because God hates women. Then Caro got even more sad so she smacked Collier across the face as hard as she could, yelling, 'My mama don't like that kind of talk, so stop it.' Then Collier hugged Caro and didn't let her go until Caro's face was dry and she had stopped shaking. And Harper stood there, just watching them.

'How come?'

'Every time shut my eyes, I see her,' Tillie says. 'And I aint tryin to see no one after they're dead.'

147

'Me too.'

'How's that?'

'God hates women. It's why He lets them die all the time,' Harper says.

Tillie passes the joint from her right hand to her left and pops Harper in the back of the head. 'Don't be sayin that blasphemous shit. I don't care where you been, girl—yaint speakin like that in front of me. I don't like that kinda talk.'

Harper smiles and Tillie smacks her across the face with a hard, flat palm. 'Somethin funny?'

'No, m'am.' Her smile settles low on her face and she doesn't have the urge to laugh anymore. 'I'm sorry.'

'That's better,' Tillie says and lights the joint.

Harper smiles to herself as Tillie's stinging touch fades.

'I keep my hand flat because I love you.'

'Yes, m'am.'

'Who you see? Who you see when you close your eyes?' Tillie inhales for three Mississippis then hands the joint to Harper.

'Nah,' Harper says, shaking her head.

'Gone, it's for medicinal purposes.'

Harper smiles. 'Aint sick.'

'You got your own sick to worry about—now, who you see?' Tillie says again.

Harper inhales as long as she can then watches the smoke from the lit tip rise and swirl in front of her. She exhales.

'Just this uh, girl, well, woman I guess. Just this woman I know.'

'Oh,' Tillie says, rocking, 'she nice?'

'No.'

'I know her?'

'She's a murdereress.'

Tillie laughs and coughs as Harper passes the joint back. 'I know plenty of murderesses. Tell me bout yours.'

Harper squints into the sun. 'She aint mine and I aint like her. I aint nothin like her.'

148

'She treat you all right?'

'I guess.' Harper picks at the broken boards of the steps and a small splinter slides under her fingernail. 'Dammit.'

'Good,' Tillie says, taking another long hit.

Harper shrugs and picks at the splinter lodged in her finger.

'What happen last night?' Tillie hacks, loosening the poisonous phlegm living in her throat. She hands Harper the joint. 'You gone tell me what happen?'

'Nope,' Harper replies.

'He breathin when yall left?'

'I think so.'

'Be careful with that kinda shit. The liver and heart in that damn idiot bout to give. He'll be gone soon enough by his own means.'

'Boys don't never die,' Harper says. 'But he won't say nothin, he'd never say it was us. Couldn't bear to have people know it was us. I can't wait till he's dead.'

'Me too,' Tillie says. 'Where this reefer come from?'

'Dunno.'

'Good answer,' she says, smiling the best she can. 'You angry bout things?'

'Nope.'

'It's the quiet ones—quiet ones who the most angry, the ones to worry bout.'

'Aint angry. I aint nothin.'

'You allowed to be.'

'Caro—she uh, she's different.'

'She grew up a bit.'

'She's awful smart.'

'You know right after you left, she had take these—those booze classes and all that. She was real shaken up. Think all of it scared her just right. You leavin scared her and made her real angry.'

'Angry at who?'

'Herself. Collier. You.'

149

'Collier's the same but that aint Caro's fault, nothin's Caro's fault—'

'You shackled to your Mama but Collier and Caro shackled themselves to you. You went for all of them.'

Harper says nothing.

'You helped her, you helped Caro. You did. Just a shame Caro the only one who took the help you gave. I know why you did it but I'm still sad you did.'

'Caro's smart on her own.'

'You saved Caro's life and it's all right if you're angry. Bein angry is fine. But sulkin around, havin a pity party for yourself won't do. Yaint no leper, not more'n any other woman. Be angry if you want but don't pout and stop pillin.'

Harper says nothing.

'Never thought of yall as trouble. Yall got into the garbage most kids do I guess. Runnin around, bein a bit reckless. Thing is folks don't mind when it's boys doin it, carryin on.'

Harper says nothing.

'Things be better for Caro if I was gone. I keep her here.'

'Don't say that.'

'I know yall don't get on but your daddy did you a favour by gettin your Mama outta here. He shouldn't done it like he did, but he's givin you a chance, Harper.'

'He shouldn't done it like he did. She aint sick.'

'She aint sick?' Tillie says. 'Then what is it? What is She if She aint sick?'

'She's tired.'

'Tired like you is? That's the type a tired get you sent where She is. And you don't belong there.'

'Neither do She.'

Tillie sighs. 'Your Mama, She's havin a bad spell is all. Still, yaint tired like Her and yaint sick like Her.'

Harper says nothing.

'She's having a bad spell is all. It'll pass—pass in time like the others did.'

'But they always come back, don't they? Like all the other spells. She must be a witch cause all She got is spells. Her spells. Her spells always swim back to Her.'

'We got knocked up round a same time. Bart used to have these real big field parties in the summer when the sun got low. She'd come out, your Mama, come out in the field and dance circles round your daddy. He always wear them button down shirts, church shirts. He never take his eyes off Her. He fell in love with Her in Bart's field. Started with him trailin after his older brothers who always lookin for trash that put out. But She was different. Your Mama always been real beautiful, She just didn't know what to do with Herself. Missed Her when I left a while back—to go have Caro down in Lake Providence to be with her daddy—Dennis Naylor who got dicks for brains. But I came back here cause of your Mama.'

And there are no more words until there are.

'Sorry,' Harper says in Tillie's silence.

'What for?'

'That you had to come back.'

'Me too. But your daddy could have left. Coulda left a long time ago but he didn't.'

'He's fuckin pathetic. He's sad.'

'He just jealous is all.'

'Jealous of what?'

'Jealous you and Her got out of here before he had the chance to.'

'We didn't have the chance for nothin.'

'Stop feelin sorry for yourself—yall got a taste for not bein here. Don't matter where you was, it was somewhere he aint never been. He's scared a yall, what yall know about things now. He's scared yall stronger than he is.'

'We are.'

'I know it.' Tillie smiles something wonderful like a secret is melting on her tongue. 'Caro—Caro's a bit different now but I know she loves Olivia only half as much as she loves you.'

'I'm tired.'

'Yaint the only one.' Tillie stands and then takes Harper's hands in her own, brings them to her lips and kisses them. The finger with the splinter throbs.

'You got hands like your Mama,' Tillie says and kisses them again. 'And your Mama has God in those hands a Hers.'

Six and Eight

'It's too hot,' Harper yells.

'Girl, it's always too hot,' She says with Her head tipped back and the glass pressed to her forehead underneath the midday sun.

'I'm bored,' Harper says, sitting in the driveway with sweaty handfuls of drawing chalk. 'I said I'm bored.'

'Why the hell you bored?' She calls from the porch. 'Draw your Mama a picture of somethin, draw a nice picture for me with the chalk.'

'Don't wanna.'

'Well then sweetheart, yaint bored. You lazy.'

'Aint lazy,' Harper says, dragging a piece of pink chalk from an oil stain to a chunk of broken tar.

'Hey, come here,' She says, setting Her glass onto the banister. She trips, but catches Herself on the porch railing. Settling into the grass, She crosses Her legs and Her shorts ride up Her thighs. She reaches for Harper who sits in front of Her, crossing her own legs. Their knees touch. 'See my hand here?' She opens Her palm and holds it an inch from Harper's face. 'What's it say?'

Harper places a finger just below Her wedding ring and traces a crease across Her palm, trailing down to Her wrist.

'Hands say things. Can tell a whole person's past and even a whole person's life, things that aint even happen yet, by what they got written on their hands.'

'Yeah?'

'Course you can. See this one time, me and your daddy had to drive across the whole damn state to go see his piece of shit mama. And since I aint never been anywhere but here, I told him to drive real slow through the places I never seen. So we're drivin and I see this little shack all busted and broken, plywood boardin up the windows, but it had this sign out front that it was open for business. It belonged to this psychic woman, a voodoo madam. So your daddy pulls the car over and I go in—but course he won't come cause he's scared of witches—so I go in that shack and slap my dollar on the table. Then she started readin the maps God laid on my palms. And you know what she said to me?'

'What she say?' Harper's whole face holds a smile just like Hers. She grips each of Her knees as tight as she can. 'Tell me.'

'She looked at my hand then at the funny lookin cards on the table then back at me in this real crazy way and whispered real real quiet—' Her lips are so close to Harper's they can taste each other. They taste themselves in the heat. '—she said, Miss Lucy, you gone live longer than that husband a yours waitin in the car now. And you gone outlive your daddy now too.'

'Yeah?' Harper says, climbing into Her lap, straddling Her waist.

'Yep. Honest she did. Greatest thing anyone ever told me. Know what else she said?'

'What?'

'She told me I aint never gone see no angels, but I'll prolly meet a witch or two.'

'Yeah?'

'Sure did. Witches the greatest women there ever was. You a witch? You the witch I'm suppose to meet?' She pinches at Harper's hip and blows at her neck.

'No.' Harper laughs. 'Do me. Do mine. Read my hands.'

'All right,' She says, untangling Harper from Her own body and returning her to the ground. She holds Harper's hand, brings it real close to Her face and studies the little lines showing six years of her story.

'Christ Almighty, Harper. Your hands filthy. Give em a wash.'

'I'll wash them later.'

'Should make you wait till you get yourself in the tub.'

'I get in tonight.'

'Promise?'

'Yeah, promise.'

She studies her hand again. 'Look at that.'

'What? What's it say?'

With a smile cut sharp as a sickle and sweet as syrup She says, 'You gone last longer than us all. You'll be listenin to us all when we long gone but you'll never be done cause you a real strong girl like that. Girl, you gone live forever.'

Caro said she never paid mind to Tillie's hands until the wake— not until she was standing over Tillie's casket looking down at them because she couldn't stomach looking at her mama's face. Caro said there wasn't much difference between the way Tillie looked in that box and the way she looked when she was real sick. But Caro says in her memories Tillie's never sick.

Caro didn't say it, but I'm sure she was real mad that Tillie and Collier's funerals were only two weeks apart. Donna waited three months to bury Collier. Said she wasn't sure if the whole thing was worth the money or not, if Collier was worth the whole to-do. And Tillie died while Donna was still deciding. So then Donna asked Caro if she could recycle some of the flower arrangements from Tillie's service for Collier's. The geraniums were near dead anyways so Caro told Donna go ahead. But she said to better make sure Collier wasn't buried nowhere near Tillie.

Caro told me she went to Collier's service but not her burial. And that after the service she watched eleven people file from the church to the cemetery while she walked home with her eyes fixed on the pavement and a cigarette in her hand. The first time I asked Caro if she cried at Collier's funeral she said she did even though I wasn't there to stab or pinch her. But then Caro said her crying was more leftover tears from Tillie's funeral than about being sad for Collier. Caro will always be a shit liar. Sometimes I think the only person who loved Collier more than me was Caro. But I'm the best liar of us all.

Caro said I'm a coward for not coming and that if I really wanted to know about the funerals I would have found a way to come myself because a halfway house isn't a prison. Then she said I'm lazy and I'm scared. Then she said she's sorry. Always. But that first time I ever asked her, she told me she saw you at both. That you kissed her at both. That you held and hugged her while you told her she looked really pretty. Thank you for doing what you did.

Caro called Collier's funeral a procession of the lame, which is an awful thing to say. The worst part is, Caro's right because I'm sure it was. Almost everybody was surprised she lasted as long as she did. Caro and me are the only ones who remember Collier. It's best this way.

It's funny how Collier made me feel safe in a way Caro couldn't. Guess it's funny seeing that Collier could be pretty dangerous when she wanted to be—when everything she touched turned to fire then ash then nothing. Took Caro a real long while to figure out that she needed to save herself before she saved me or anyone else. Still, she was stubborn, and she tried to help me as long as she could.

Nineteen, Nineteen and Twenty-One

Caro wipes each wet glass dry and sets it on the rack under the bar top. A loose black apron string hangs from each hip and when she catches Harper's glance, she smiles the best she can, before returning to the glasses.

'Only reason you even here, Harper,' Cain Lowell says, taking the time to spit his dip into an empty mug Caro has just washed clean, 'cause Caro's leavin soon for school.' Caro dries her hands on a dingy Budweiser towel then folds her arms across her chest.

The damp walls of the bar are hidden underneath newspaper clippings, old baseball cards and All-Star county pennants. A signed picture of Ralph Sampson from his last All-American season hangs next to a marriage announcement of another child bride. The corners of the clipping are curling. There's a picture of Tommy playing at FSU—tan, wearing his white uniform with crimson and gold stitching and holding a bat outstretched like he's just hit the ball. He looks so pretty because he is.

'Harper, you hear me?' Cain says.

'Yeah.'

'Aint hard—work easy enough girls can do it. Just serve drinks and clean up after. Clean up a bit when you get here and before you leave at night.'

'Okay.'

'Yaint old enough to drink now.'

'Yeah, I know.'

'Let me catch you, let me catch you just once and I call Bart and them. You on parole aintcha?'

'Yessir.'

'Be good and it goes by real quick. Trust me—my parole flew by cause I was good like I suppose to be.' Black juice spills from his bottom lip and he spits into the mug again. 'So don't be drinkin behind the bar and don't be cursin too much neither cause folks don't like that when they tryin to have a nice time. Don't be tellin people you work here neither. If anyone asks, tell them you helpin out for a bit and that's all.'

'Okay.'

'Got questions, you ask Caro.'

'How much am I makin?'

'You makin what everyone else makin.'

'What's that?'

'Bout four dollars an hour.'

'What about tips?'

'You make them, you can keep them. Gone then, work with Caro till we close up. And Harper—'

'Yeah?'

'Pull your hair outcha your face, boys like that—when they can see ya face. Aintcha Mama ever tell you that?'

'Too much,' Harper says when foam spills over the lip of the pitcher onto her hands.

'Here, you have to tip it like this.' Caro places her hands on Harper's so they're grabbing the handle together. Caro turns the pitcher on its side, away from her, and levels out as beer rises before she flips the draft spigot back. 'Perfect,' she says, setting it onto the bar top. She smiles and slides it along with an empty glass to Noah Scott. He hands her a five-dollar bill. She punches numbers on the cash register and the drawer pops open. Caro makes change and shuts the drawer with her hip before returning bills and coins to Noah's upturned palm. He winks at her and she does a good job smiling back at him. 'If someone's had too much, cut them off.'

'How much is too much?'

'You tell me.'

'I dunno how much too much is,' Harper says.

'You can thank your Mama for that. Just—listen. Everything here is really easy, it is. Just be nice.'

'I am—I will be.'

'Be nice,' Caro says again.

'I will.'

'Can't serve Tommy or Collier.'

'How come?'

'Cain doesn't want them served here and it's his place. Oh, be sure to wipe the taps after you use them.' Caro runs a damp rag over the spigots leaving them polished.

'Why?' Harper asks. 'Collier aint his mama.'

'Well, cause—because she doesn't ever come here alone.

Collier doesn't do anything alone. Collier can't be alone, you know that.'

A thick hardback book with newspaper-looking print on the cover sits next to a stack of empty pitchers. Harper brushes her fingers along the well-broken spine: *The Reagan Years*. She opens the book and sifts through the real shiny pages of real shiny men with real shiny smiles.

'Want to quiz me?' Caro asks, taking a handful of peanuts from the dish and dumping them into her mouth.

Nineteen, Nineteen and Twenty-One

'Women born sinners,' Tara Hackett says with her fingers intertwined behind her head. Her body is lying straight on the bed and looks like a rotten two-by-four forgotten during a rainy month. 'Just tell them what they wanna hear is all. Tell them they saved you. Tell them you learned your lesson. Tell them you aint no threat. Tell them you earned parole.'

Harper stands at the sink, brushing the teeth in the very back of her mouth foaming blue and white bubbles. Foam like a mad dog. Foam like a mad girl. She's scrubbing so hard, her gums bleed. She spits into the sink, pink marbles down the drain.

'Say what they want and smile. Smile on account they saved you. But don't smile too much. Don't show teeth. Dogs doin that when they're scared. You show all your pretty teeth, they think you're scared and that you're lyin. Don't wear red neither, only whores wear red.'

Standing behind Harper, Tara Hackett tugs at the red dress Sister Paul gave Harper to wear.

'That aint true.'

'Sure goddam is, Mary Magdalene. You let a nigger save you, huh?'

Harper says nothing.

'Now ask me.'

158

'Ask you what?'

'You didn't ask me if you can wear this dress. Now ask me like a good girl do.'

Harper says nothing.

'Say it.'

Blood collects in the fleshy gutter between her teeth and lip and she swallows rust before spitting pink and red into the sink. 'May I wear this dress, m'am?'

'You look like a fuckin whore. Your Mama be so proud.'

Harper's gaze falls to the concrete floor and then rises to the white streaks of her scarred knees peeking out from underneath the hem of the recycled dress.

'Tell them what you wanna be when you grow up.' Tara Hackett's face floats next to Harper's in the mirror. 'What you wanna be when you grow up, girl?'

'Dunno,' Harper replies. Her gums are raw.

'Give them somethin. Give them a lie. Give them the truth. Don't matter a damn bit. Just give them somethin to swallow.'

'When I grow up I'll be somebody's mama,' Harper says.

'Liar.' Tara Hackett cackles and presses her teeth to the back of Harper's neck.

The guard beats his baton against the cell wall three times. 'Yall cut that shit out.'

Sister Josephine Paul stands next to him with her lips moving in silence and she just stands there, praying behind the glass with her eyes open.

'You look at that nigger again and I fuckin cut your tongue out—you hear me?'

Harper looks into the mirror again and watches Tara Hackett's dry lips twitch.

'You be fine.' Tara Hackett whispers just like she does when it's dark. 'You a sweet girl so me and God gone free you.'

159

Nineteen, Nineteen and Twenty-One

'Going home for dinner. I'll be back soon. You okay?' Caro says.

'Yeah,' Harper says, dumping more peanuts into a shallow dish and handing them to Lot Dull who sits on the stool closest to the TV.

'Heard you back,' Lot says.

'Yeah.'

'Good girl. First bit is the hardest, get past at—you'll be fine. Just remember to stay out. Took me couple trips to learn.' He palms a small handful of peanuts and pours them into his mouth. 'You at your daddy's?'

'For now.'

'Good girl. You let me know if you ever need anythin.'

'Thank you,' Harper says.

'Hey, your Mama dead yet?'

'No, sir.'

'Well that's good to hear. Let me get a shot and a beer. Turn that up while you at it.' Lot gestures towards the TV.

Two fingers of thick amber fill the glass tumbler and smells like Caro's breath when she suddenly feels like telling secrets, saying things out loud that she shouldn't. Harper fills a mug like Caro does then sets the two glasses in front of Lot.

'Tony Gwynn aint half what Kirby Puckett was. Gone,' he says taking a long draw from his beer, 'pour one for yourself too.'

'I'm all right.'

'Sure?'

She nods.

'Who yall like in your daddy's house?'

'Baltimore.'

'That's right. Ripken done all right this season.' The tattooed anchors and topless tits painted on Lot's right forearm are bleeding.

'Yeah, and he still aint missed a game yet.'

160

Lot smiles. 'Yeah, he is. Lucky girl, we didn't have no TV when I was in.'

'Lucky girl,' she says.

'He's pretty tall to be playin middle of the field.'

'Nah, he aint no taller than Andres Thomas was.'

'He few inches taller than Andres Thomas.'

'Andres Thomas was shit,' Harper says. 'Ripken aint that tall.'

Lot's bourbon empties with a quick pull. Harper fills it then returns it to him. 'Thanks, sweetheart. He only been thrown out once before, you know that?' Lot takes a long sip, the glass held by a large, leathery hand that's marked in the same white paint that covers his shirt and jeans. He's stained in sweat and paint and bourbon and sun and something else that could be mustard. 'Hey, look at him.' Lot grabs Harper's arm with his long, paint-covered fingers and holds her steady. 'Just look at him there, Ripken got too long legs for a shortstop. Just look at him.' He's pointing at the screen still and his eyes are real glassy, straining towards the television. He drains his beer. Harper rinses the empty mug and places it in the washer.

'Look at you, real quick on the uptake. You'll do good,' Lot says. 'Back to work. Shit don't paint itself, do it?'

Lot hands Harper a ten-dollar bill. She punches the register keys same as Caro and the drawer slides open. She takes her time carefully counting the change.

'Gone, you keep it. Have a good one, sweetheart,' he calls, walking through the back door.

Harper smiles to herself, shoving the dollars into her pocket. Noah Scott is the only person in the bar and he's so drunk he doesn't know if it's day or night. Harper turns her back to him and quickly guzzles the rest of Lot's bourbon before tossing the glass into the sink.

'Afternoon, Harper.' Pastor Jim sits on Lot's barstool underneath the glisten of an overhead light giving himself that barely-there halo he likes so much. Dressed in a pressed

161

seersucker suit with his slick hair dripping dark jelly tracks down the back of his neck, he smells like fresh Christmas trees or the type of gin that rich people probably drink.

'Afternoon, sir.' Harper hugs herself around the waist, pulling herself in tight, pulling herself away from him and not showing him any teeth.

'See you found yourself some work then. Now that's real good,' he says, tugging at the white cuffs of his shirtsleeves. 'Doin your part.'

'Yessir.'

'Lot of bottles, huh?'

Harper says nothing.

'Temptation a mighty powerful thing.' He runs a plastic broken-tooth comb through his wet-looking hair. 'When a lost lamb of the Lord surrounds himself with sin like this, takes a real heavy strength from the Father to turn away from the will of Satan.'

The top of the bourbon bottle spins as she opens it. She pours with a loose grip then caps the bottle shut. Emptying the glass in two swallows, she then places the glass onto the bar top. 'Good thing I'm a person and aint no sheep then.'

He smiles real big, forces a laugh and looks at her, but not into her. She won't let him.

'You the spittin image of your Mama,' he says. 'You know that? You miss Her?'

'Almost as much as you miss sellin Her dope.'

'Sound like Her too and I hear you just as thirsty—'

'Why you here if you aint thirsty?'

'Lord gave me strength to get off the bottle years ago. He'll save a prisoner if you let Him, Harper. He can even save you—matter a fact, He save trash all the time. Just let Him into that heart a yours.'

'I'm sure He got better places to be.'

'Got sass like your Mama too,' he says, leaning on his forearms.

'You aint the first to say that.' Harper wrings a dry bar towel in her hands, drawing it taut as a bat and letting her arms hang, locked straight, at her sides. 'Yaint special.'

'Maybe I aint. But the Lord is the only one I'm answering to. Not some booze slinging piece a trash.' He speaks so the only ones who can hear him are Harper and his God and her devil.

'You gone save me then?' Harper says. 'Better pray harder.'

'No.' He gives a twist to each of his cufflinks, calming himself in their gold touch. 'Need to talk to your daddy.'

'He don't spend his afternoons in bars. He got himself a job, sir.'

'It's just that—' he starts speaking louder, 'the elders wonderin if he gone make a donation to the buildin fund like the rest of his brothers in the community done.'

'Buildin fund of what?'

'We givin a lift to the sanctuary, givin it new bones.'

'Yall don't need his money for that.'

'*And they came, both men and women, as many as were willin hearted, and brought bracelets, and earrings, and rings, and tablets, all jewels of gold: and every man that offered an offerin of gold unto the Lord.*'

'*You ask and do not receive cause you ask amiss that you may spend it on your pleasure,*' Harper says. 'I know some too and I bet you build three sanctuaries if you stop dippin in all the time.'

'You nothin but a lost sheep and there a long and rocky path ahead of you now, girl. You wanna go to hell, Harper? Cause you talk like it. But maybe that's where you belong, girl. You wanna spend eternity in damnation?'

'Already been. Aint that bad—they give you a wife'n a nun'n dope if you spread your legs enough.'

'You're an abomination. That's your filth, girl. You're filled with nothin but Satan.'

'Guess at makes two of us then,' Harper says.

'You best watch yourself, girl,' he hisses, 'you slippin awful fast.'

The Bible is a book written by men. The Bible is a book that seems it'll never end. Used to be I only read the Old Testament but now I read both parts—the parts with Jesus and the parts before Him. The Bible has pages thin like Tillie's skin. Turning those pages you can almost see clear through them. Have to be real careful so they won't tear because this the only Bible I have. My Bible is the only Bible in the whole house. When the girls downstairs ask to borrow it I usually say no, don't want them to rip the pages or steal it, but sometimes I say yes as long as I can watch them read it. So I sit while they read it, just sit there watching them to make sure they don't hurt it. Usually they only want to read a chapter or two about Jesus curing a blind person or the Resurrection or that water into wine part. I take it back as soon as they're done and go read it again myself. Turning from one page to another don't take too long. Turn enough pages and another day gone.

One time Tillie said time is like a morphine drip and I'm just trying my best to pass the minutes and hush the girls and their ghosts. When somebody is dead they should be silent, but just because they should be dead don't mean they are. Every day and every night and every minute I'm breathing, I hear them. I hear them and I feel their touch everywhere. They leave their stamp on me. Who they were and the things they said to me and the things they taught me and the way they raised me to be a girl who don't ever really have a chance of changing— they remind me of everything, every day.

They won't let me sleep. They make me listen, force me to hear their words while they say the things they always have. Her and Collier and Tillie and Tara Hackett and Sister Paul and Caro. Like the bunch of them a Lady Lazarus or something. Even though Caro's not dead yet, sometimes it feels like she already is. They won't let me sleep. Nothing but a cyclone of voices swirling round and round where my brain should be. They're a choir of naked bodies, their skin and their voice coming together. And if it wasn't so terrifying, maybe it could be beautiful—the type of beautiful so strong you can't look straight at it because it's too bright and hurts too much. They say that about angels in the Bible you know. A light so blaring and dangerous and beautiful it's like looking into the sun, you want to and you have to, even though you know it'll hurt you. But how they look's not what keeps me awake. Their voices spin together real fast and real tight, I can't tell the difference between who is saying what because their voices all bleed together. I can't tell one from another. I can't tell if they're witches or angels and I never sleep.

I'm tired all the time because their lips speak together. They're always speaking together. And when they speak, I can't sleep. But when I do, all I see is Sister Josephine Paul's body.

Nineteen, Nineteen and Twenty-One

'I prayed for this every day since I met you,' Sister Paul says with Harper's face in her hands. 'Good for you, girl.'

Sister Paul is smiling so hard the muscles of her face twitch. The corners of her mouth pull back towards her ears and her lips are parted. Her breath is warm and settles on Harper's face. She wraps her arms around Harper and presses her palms to Harper's shoulder blades, pulling their bodies together. She holds the curve of Harper's skull. 'Good for you, girl.'

Harper exhales, and when Paul releases her, wipes at her eye sockets with the back of her hand and steadies her gaze into Paul's eyes—they're brown with specks of green and she is the light.

'Where's the guard?' Harper says.

'I'll take you back. I'd like to.'

The corridor has walls three feet thick and a floor lined with

165

edgeless shadows. Layers of dead air fall on their bodies. The rosary hangs at Sister Paul's hip, swinging back and forth, falling into her thigh with every second stride. Harper's pulse beats steady in her throat and their fingers are intertwined as they walk down the empty concrete hallway. Paul's steps are slow and considered, her breathing is soft.

'Please don't stop prayin for my Mother and please don't stop prayin for Job—'

Harper's knees buckle when she's kicked from behind. After she rolls onto her back, a clenched fist meets her jaw in a clean hit. Lifting her dizzied head from the ground, she watches the rosary being stripped from Sister Paul's hip and wrapped twice around her neck, the worn beads branding her windpipe with fat, suffocating circles. Tara Hackett pulls the string of prayer beads tighter, her fingers turning purple as she brings Sister Paul onto her toes. Paul gropes at her neck, her eyes roll to the back of her head. She speaks to God in silence, her lips barely moving, her fingers frenzied but weak at her throat while Tara Hackett takes the rosary in one hand like wooden reins and draws them tighter.

'Shoulda prayed harder for me, nigger—' Tara Hackett's forked tongue curse echoes through the corridor as the screwdriver enters Sister Josephine Paul's throat up to its handle, the worn plastic kissing the now leaking flesh. Tara Hackett releases Paul who falls onto her knees with her head bowed, the crown of her head beneath Tara Hackett's blistered fingertips. Tara Hackett bends and pulls the screwdriver from Paul's neck and pushes it in again, claiming a new hole. A spigot of blood trails from her throat down her chest to her waist. Harper crawls to Paul and Tara Hackett's toe clips her temple. Tara Hackett spits in her face then pulls Harper's mouth to hers. 'Look at her while you sittin—sittin there doin nothin. Look at your nigger who you can't save—she just like at Mama of yours, huh? You gone kill them both, sweetheart.'

Tara Hackett straddles Paul's body then punctures the skin

between her breasts, drags the sharpened flathead in two clean slits, throat to belly then shoulder to shoulder, carving Sister Paul, branding her a woman of God and the best one of those I know is Tillie but Tillie aint here and I can taste the rot of Sister Paul, smell her decay already so I puke on the concrete floor and my hands and her eyes aren't brown with flecks of green they're all white and the tremors of her body are almost silent the pulse of her limbs fading on all fours I puke more without looking at her no more I reach for her left hand the one I been holding while three guards beat Tara Hackett with batons breaking her jaw unhinged and ugly pushing against the skin of her face to be freed from an evil host but a fractured smile still with her arms bent and locked behind her she never took her eyes off me until they pulled her to her feet Tara Hackett rises to crack her skull against the windowless walls so they both bleed in front of me but I don't touch Tara Hackett no more and press my hand to Sister Paul's chest shut my eyes tilt my head downwards whisper Tillie's words the ones I know God will hear because Tillie is right with the Lord and knows what to say her soul is good Caro's soul is good and Caro never gets caught and Collier may as well be dead She may as well be dead Sister Josephine Jo like Jo March's corpse has the touch and smell of Collier when she gets dope sick pressing my palm harder between her breasts where the two drawn cuts meet in the crux of the bloody cross her mouth is slack jawed loose and open dry dead don't gasp no more my hands painted with her blood if I hadn't watch her pass I would have thought the blood was my own they let Paul bleed out and beat Tara Hackett Collier says God hates women and now they'll all be dead.

Sister Josephine Paul choked to death on her own blood, thirsty for air. She lay there drowning, spewing wet hacks and gurgling on the very thing that gave her life and she never asked for help or fought back. She spoke to God until she expired and all I did was sit there.

Nineteen, Nineteen and Twenty-One

'How many times I tell you, don't smoke in your daddy's house,' Denise shouts, letting a too-small apron fall over her neck. She wraps it around her inflated middle and ties it behind her back.

Harper says nothing, taking the unlit cigarette from her lips to behind her ear and returns Her lighter to her pocket.

'Lookin for a job yet?' Denise washes her hands, taking her time and scrubbing the knuckle of every finger.

'What?'

'You don't need to be workin at Cain's no more. No reason you need be workin in a bar.'

'Yall told me get a job, so I did. Where else gone take me?'

'When you goin back to school?' Denise scrapes two thick slabs of butter into the pot on the stove.

Harper's eyes sting while the morning sun beats through the window, setting the linoleum floor aflame. Or maybe her eyes sting because she hasn't cried or slept in some time now. Or maybe the pills. But probably not, because like Collier said, just medicine is all.

'You sure is quiet for a change—oh, you got about a week to get over and see your Mama.'

'Why? Why a week?' Harper says, still standing in the door, just standing to take up space.

'She uh—headin to a hospital in Dallas soon.' Denise cuts carrots into thin slices. They stand on the cutting board then fall flat to their sides like small wet playing cards.

'What?'

'You even listenin to me? Ever? Christ, yaint never listen to no one.'

'I aint goddam deaf.'

'Stop takin the Lord's name in vain. Aint no need to curse and raise your voice,' Denise says with her back to Harper. 'She's movin to a new hospital that's in Dallas. How many times I got to say it? Where She's at now is gettin steep. I found

168

a hospital in Dallas that's cheaper. It'll be easier for your daddy—it aint even like ya wanna see Her. You aint even been out there yet.'

'They do terrible shit to women in those cheap ass shitholes—they do. Pump em full of drugs they don't need, make em junkies and then doctors do awful to them and they can't even say nothin about it. Why you sendin Her somewhere like that? What happen to his money? You said he had a promotion. You the one who said that.'

'Other things need tendin now.' The skin of Denise's knuckles is pulled tight, making her bones easy to see.

'Like what?'

'We just tryin to do our part. I'm tellin you how things is and how they gone be cause no one else will.' Denise keeps her back to Harper. She's still cutting carrots, her posture lazy, weight settled in her lower back giving her a slight hunch over the counter.

'Yaint got nothin to do with their money.'

'Their money? Your Mama aint worked a goddam day in her life. Your daddy and me just tryin to do our part—don't you ever listen? We're helpin give the sanctuary new bones, we're doing our part.'

'Layin with your Sister's husband so you can build a sin box. You must be real proud,' Harper says, talking fast because that's what Collier's communion makes you do. Talk fast and tell the truth.

'Watch your mouth, if you was mine—'

Harper clicks her tongue, tasting the drip at the back of her throat. 'She's your own Sister. You're a real piece a shit. She's your fuckin Sister—'

'She aint shit, when you gone see that? She aint never gettin better, She aint never gonna change. She always gone be what She is. She a drunk whore who don't know when to shut up. She's trash and She passed on what She is to you. And guess what, sweetheart? Your Mama gone die one day, prolly real

169

soon cause God is tired of dealin with Her shit. She gone die and when that happen then, whatcha gone have then?'

'You a stray that rubs on him when he's sad—that's what you are to him. You a stray. You know that?'

'Yaint even worth no slap. Could beat the shit outta you but it won't make no difference. You aint worth the time it takes to raise a hand—you just like Her—I'm gonna tell you a secret, sweetheart—I prayed every night some dyke kill you because it'll only take one of you to stop breathin to make both yall die.'

Harper grabs her by the throat, her pulse underneath her fingertips. Pushing Denise down onto her knees, Harper feels the ridges of her vocal cords.

'You wanna see your Mama so bad, look in the mirror, girl.' Denise's knees rub against the just cleaned linoleum while she's groping and swinging and scratching at Harper's arms. Harper squeezes harder, pressing both thumbs into her windpipe. Denise's fat limbs flail, her arms useless and pathetic.

Luke jerks Harper's arm back so hard it nearly pops out of its socket. He tosses her out of the kitchen and into the living room. Harper falls to the stained carpet and laughs.

'Hell's wrong with you?' he says, standing over her.

Harper pushes herself up from the floor and lunges at Denise again but Luke catches her by the neck this time, his long fingers grasping Her flesh and pinning Her against the wall. His face is red and his dark pupils are real small like still black marbles. His palm is soft, his grip firm—holding Her so tight She wonders if he's afraid to let Her go, thinking this might be the last time he ever touches Her. The last time he'll ever touch Her. He's afraid to let Her go, Harper thinks. That's it. That must be it. He's afraid to let Them go.

'Feel good, don't it?' Harper smirks.

'When you gone learn?' He hooks his right thumb into Her left eye socket pulling the eyelid up. His dark marbles peer real close into Hers. 'You high?'

Harper can feel Her swimming in her stomach, creeping up her throat and scraping against her fleshy insides, clawing to get out. 'Cmon, I won't even fight back. Take a shot, you earned it.'

'Yaint never gone learn.' He's the saddest looking boy pretending to be a man there ever was.

'Know why you aint never been to see Her? You don't gotta, do you? You got me,' Harper says. 'You wanna have at me? Ask pretty and maybe I'll let you, daddy.'

He pulls Her towards him and pushes Her back into the wall. There's a real sharp pain at the base of Her skull.

'Be nice, daddy. You know how still I had to lay to get back to you?'

'Get outta here fore I call Bart,' he says, his breath leaking into her mouth.

'You don't scare me, you coward, you cunt.'

He releases Her neck as his closed fist crosses Her face. His skin on hers burns sweaty and raw. He could have gone harder if he wanted to—could have gone harder if he let himself be a man and not a little boy. He could have if he just let himself not be so weak.

The ripped screen door, still in desperate need of mending, is the only thing separating Harper and Tillie.

'Take me to see Her.'

'Jesus.' A dead cigarette hangs from Tillie's lips, casting a small thin shadow on her chin. When she gently palms her jaw, Harpers flinches.

'Take me to Her.'

'You got no business over there.'

'Take me to see Her. Tillie, please. Take me to Her.'

'You don't need no one take you nowhere. You need take your own self somewhere. Take yourself somewhere, cause time's comin for you when the rot can't rot no more.'

'Caro can take me to see Her then.'

'You too clever to be doin such stupid shit all the time.'

'Maybe I ought pray more.'

'You look real ugly when you lie. You know that?' Tillie says.

'Where's Caro?'

Tillie sighs and relights her cigarette. She pushes the door open, even though Harper could have stepped clean through the screen.

'Harper, you stupid as shit sometimes. Cmon, she in the back.'

'This our exit?' Caro says, pulling down the sun visor.

'Nah,' Harper says.

'You sure? See, look.' She points to a green sign with white letters. 'Valley Memorial, Exit 118, Keep Right. Look.'

'Keep on straight.'

Caro's eyes shift in the rearview mirror. 'We should get off the highway up here where it says to. You've never even been there. I've been there lots of times.'

'We aint gettin off here—we aint done yet.' Harper places her hand on Caro's wrist, tight enough to make sure the car keeps straight but loose enough not to leave a mark. Harper holds Caro holding the steering wheel. 'We're going forty-seven miles in a straight line. Then, when I tell you—when I say you can—then, you get off at the exit after at Dairy Queen sign. You hear me, Carolyn?'

Caro bites her bottom lip so hard it's almost purple.

'Hey, it's okay,' Harper says gently, gripping the back of Caro's neck and pulling her head in close. 'Cmon, it's fine. You been out here loads of times. Don't gotta come in or nothin. Just wait. You just wait for me.'

'I'm so tired of waiting for you.'

A bit of concrete from the road flies into the windshield and leaves a small debit in the glass. The crack doesn't spread. Glass pushes against itself, holding itself together to keep from falling. But the crack is still there even though the glass doesn't shatter.

'I don't wanna go,' Caro says, quietly. 'I told you I don't ever wanna go there again.'

'Collier aint scared a nothin.'

'That's because Collier don't have a single thing to lose, now does she?' Caro won't look at Harper. 'That's the real reason she's not scared of anything. She has no reason to be.'

'Jesus, Caro, knock it off—don't be like that.' Harper softly pinches at her rib and Caro pushes her away.

'Stop.'

'I will—I'll stop if you say it and you mean it. Mean somethin, Caro, for once. Say somethin and mean it. You a shit liar—you always have been and you always will be.'

'Don't touch me.'

'Tell me a secret, Caro. Tell me somethin you only tell God at night.'

'I fucking hate Ann-Collier,' Caro says, real quiet, real flat, with her eyes still on the road. 'I hate her more than I could ever love anyone.'

'Good girl,' Harper says, flicking on the radio. Caro slaps her hand away and turns it off.

'Why? Please—just—why you have to go and do something like this? You don't have to be there anymore.' The engine slows, dropping to a low hum as Caro's foot leaves the gas pedal and they coast. Her foot is still, the car's speed falling quickly.

'Whatcha doin now? Cmon, quicker we get there, quicker we leave,' Harper says. 'I mean Jesus, aint nothin gone happen. You gone sit in the car twenty minutes. Read one of your books, why don't you? Twenty minutes all I'm askin for. Can you gimme that?'

'What if I'm not waiting for you when you're ready? What if I already left? What if it's me leaving you now?'

'Chrissake, leave then. Drop me off then go home. Gone. I'm not forcin you to do nothin. Sick of you whinin all the time. Pull over, let me out.' Harper reaches for the steering wheel and Caro jerks away, turning the car with her. They swerve towards the dirt and rock-ridden bank of the road.

'Don't be stupid,' Caro says, squinting into the sun. If she had a cigarette in her mouth, Harper would have sworn it was Tillie driving and bitching behind the wheel.

'Pull over I said, let me out.'

'No.'

'Why?' Harper says.

'I'm not leaving you on the side of the road.' Caro just keeps staring into the sun. Maybe she's waiting to be blinded. Daring God to let the sun take away her eyes so she won't have to be a witness anymore.

'It'll be quick,' Harper says.

'That's what you said last time.'

'Won't never ask you for nothin again. I swear, Caro. Honest. I swear.'

That was the chance to see Her, but I didn't take it. I figure that the next weekend She sat on a bus with some nurse for nearly 1700 miles while they carted Her off to a new ward. I didn't go and see Her because I didn't need to. I could see Her whenever I wanted, same as now. When I look in a mirror or when I close my eyes. I see Her in every tile of a kitchen floor, every scratch on a record, every stitch in the hem of that dress Tillie told me to burn. Every sip I have ever taken tastes of Her. It wasn't about seeing Her flesh. I guess it's more about feeling Her, because feeling things reminds me I'm not dead yet. It's about hearing Her voice and knowing that my flesh is Hers. My flesh is Her.

I didn't take the chance to see Her that day Caro drove me so the last time I seen Her was at my sentencing. 'Don't pout,' She had said to me while she balanced you on Her hip in the courtroom. 'Don't pay mind to what nobody say—you'll get back to me again. I'll get you back again. Don't pay mind to no one. Now gone—' She had said, shoving you into my face,

174

'give your brother a kiss. Tell him you love him. Tell him you real sorry for leaving.' I did all those things and you just looked at me, bald and unblinking. You wrapped your arms round Her neck and buried your face into Her. I never been so jealous of anyone in my whole life.

'Should be me going,' She had said, losing Her grip and nearly dropping you. Again. She set you on one of those wooden pews the reporters and people from round town sat in during my trial. 'Look here, look at me, Harper.' She hooked Her arm round my neck and pulled me in, Her collarbone poking my ear. 'You be okay, you be fine. You a strong girl. Don't feel bad about nothing that happened. It's okay. It is. It's okay what you done. You just trying to help your Mama is all. God gone remember this—he loves girls who help their Mama.' Her lips were pressed to my ear and Her breath was like it always was.

Felt Her eyes on me when the guard led me out of the courtroom. I didn't turn round to look at Her. Probably should have—seeing as it would have been the last time I laid eyes on Her because when Caro and me got into Tillie's car, I made her drive me to see Tara Hackett instead of going to Her hospital. I didn't know for a long time why I made Caro do that. Now I figure I wanted to see how she was getting on without me. Wanted to see if she hated me or if she still loved me or if she hurt or if she was sorry about Sister Paul or if she ached or if she was rotting or if God had forgiven her even after all the terrible things she done.

Thirty-Three and Thirty-Three

The phone rings at noon on Sunday like every Sunday and Jenny screeches Harper's name from the kitchen like every Sunday at noon then drops the receiver, letting the cord hang loose from the wall.

'How're you?'

'Well. I'm well. How are you?'

'I'm all right.'

'Good. How do you feel?

'All right.'

'You clean?'

'Twenty-three days.'

'Good for you.' Caro pauses. 'Do you still look like Her?'

'Dunno.'

'What do you mean you don't know?'

'Dunno. Haven't caught myself in mirror in a while. Your kids look like you?'

'I guess so. They look more like their daddy though. You get those pictures I sent?'

'Yeah.'

'What do you think?'

'Yeah, I think they do. Specially the one with darker hair. You look good too.'

'Kathy made me fat. I didn't gain no weight with Lynne though.'

'Shut up you aint fat, you look good.'

'You hear about Tommy?"

'No.'

'Well—'

'Don't. I don't care what happen to him.'

'You just jealous you didn't get to do it yourself.' Caro pauses. 'You uh—you need anything?'

'No.'

'You don't tell me anymore. You need to tell me what I can do. I mean it.'

'How's work?'

Caro sighs. 'It's summer. No school.'

'Oh, yeah. Yall gone vacation?'

'Might go down to Myrtle Beach.'

'Awful fancy. Look at you, fuckin rich girl.'

'Jesus, we aint rich. Shut up.'

They say nothing.

'Don't have to call here if you don't want to, Caro. Aint nobody forcin you.'

'You don't have to pick up the phone if you don't want to. No one is forcing you.'

'I know.'

Caro says nothing.

'Is it hot where you at?'

'Yeah, different kind of hot though.'

'How you mean?'

'It's a swamp.'

'Oh.'

'It's not that bad here. Not as bad as you think.'

'Is it better?'

'Better than what?'

'Better than how home got.'

'Nothing got bad, everything just stayed the same. Everything was always what it was. You just got more blind.'

'You angry, Caro?'

'No, are you?'

'No.'

'I should go then. I have to get the kids to the doctor.'

'Be good, Caro.'

'You be good.'

'I love you.'

'I love you too, Harper.'

I don't remember when Caro started running towards the things that I was running away from. Caro made herself into some stranger by the time I came back. And right before the next time I left, the time I left for good, she was the angriest person I've ever known. Caro got hard behind her eyes and kept getting harder the older we got. Caro used to say that She had been right, that Collier was nothing but a stray. But the thing Caro hated most was knowing that Collier pitied her. 'Normal for assholes, so you enjoy the harvest,' was the last thing Collier said to Caro, that same day she fell asleep on Tillie's bathroom floor.

Caro says she'll never forgive Collier for what she did to Tillie—making her find her like that and bless her like that and touch her dead body like that because Tillie loved Collier in the way only me and Caro knew. Caro said she's never been to Collier's graveside and never will because we already given her too much. 'I hate her more than I could ever love anyone,' Caro had said that day in the car but I know Caro was lying. Caro's a liar and the only person she's scared of is herself. The thing Caro is most scared of is becoming Collier, becoming like her. Her kind. Collier knew who and what she was when she died. And Caro's just jealous because she still don't have a clue who she is, and probably never will.

Nineteen, Nineteen and Twenty-One

'You know how it works—you got ten minutes. Have a seat. They bring her through.'

'Ten?' Harper asks. 'We get twenty.'

'Sit the hell down or get out,' he says, pushing her to the chair with his gun strapped tight in its holster and pressed to his waist. 'The high priestess of death row get ten minutes. Now sit cause it start now, princess.'

The glass is smeared with the fingerprints of the desperate idiots who think that just because you touch something it's real. Harper watches her own palm meet the glass, then quickly retreat into her lap.

Two guards lead her in by her wrists. She sits in the chair opposite Harper with the glass between them. Tara Hackett is fuller. It's hard to see her cheekbones under the puffy skin of her face. She's inflating, plump and soft. She's filling. Her blue jumpsuit pulls tight around her arms, tits and stomach. Buttons pull against their holes, waiting to pop and the pressure to release. Her skin is the colour of bone—looks like it has the touch and feel of putty. Like she's scared of the sun. Her normally dark eyes are light, gentle and blank. Tara Hackett's eyes are wide open but Harper knows she's sleeping. Tara Hackett picks up her phone, so Harper picks up hers.

'Well look here,' Tara Hackett says with a smile that shows all her teeth.

Harper says nothing.

'Didn't expect to see you so soon. Come to think of it, didn't expect to see you never.' Tara Hackett laughs and her face strains with her mouth hung open. Harper can see all her fillings. 'Jesus, when's the last time you had a bath? You look like shit. You know that?'

Harper says nothing.

'But hey, look at you, girl. Sittin up all straight and proud. You prolly pray now too. You still got whore in you but always been such a polite girl. Must have been raised by real fine folks. Church-goin folks and a Mama who's right with the Lord. Aint that right? God loves the Haleys.'

'You high or somethin?' Harper asks, her voice and eyes real low.

'Just a taste.'

Tara Hackett's eyes are empty. Tara Hackett's eyes are empty but heavy at the same time, like they're about to spill out of their sockets. 'You can't afford what I get these days.'

'Whatcha mean?' Harper says.

'Make me see them doctors now. Nothin but shots that make me fat. Only good thing is everythin's okay now.'

'Whatcha mean?'

'Everythin happens real soft now, nothin hurts no more.'

'Whatcha mean? Why they do all this to you? You sick?'

'Nah. But don't gotta feel sick to be sick. You and that Mama of yours should know that.'

'Do you need it—what they give you?'

'It's quiet now. Everythin's quiet. You should try it, sweetheart. Might start likin it, might even start likin yourself.' The only parts that haven't ballooned are her wrists. Almost delicate, still thin and knobby, Harper can't take her gaze off them. Tara Hackett doesn't blink or smile. Just sits still in her own stretched and flabby flesh. Just taking up space. 'Why you here, girl?'

'I dunno.'

'I dunno neither, sweetheart. I got no answers for you but guess what?'

'What?'

'I'm gettin the chair.'

'Don't say shit like that.'

'Why? It's true. You swellin yet? You somebody's mama yet? Got yourself a boyfriend?'

'No,' Harper says.

'Who you share blankets with now?'

'No one.'

'Liar.' Tara Hackett almost smiles. 'Yaint mine no more. Fuck or don't fuck whoever you want, sweetheart.'

'I can't wait till you're dead.' The truth is sweet and slick, warming Harper's lips as the words rise.

'That makes two of us.'

'Yaint gettin the chair,' Harper says.

'Sure I am.'

'You're gettin the needle.'

'Seen your Mama yet?'

Harper says nothing.

'Why not then?'

'My aunt—she uh, she's with my daddy now.'

'You jealous or somethin?'

'No.'

'You should get some sleep. Lookin real tired in your eyes and that skin looks like you been real thirsty.'

'I aint been drinkin.'

'Oh girl, you a liar. Say somethin true for once in your life. Gone—'

'I—I see, see her—I see Sister Paul every day,' Harper says real quiet into the mouthpiece. 'On the backs of my eyelids. I see her. And I see you.'

'You just laid there—laid there on the ground. You remember that? You fuckin laid there, but don't be sad, sweetheart. It was for the best, huh?'

'I wish I could put the needle in you myself.'

Tara Hackett says nothing.

'You're quiet now—your voice is quiet. You're different. Everybody's different.'

'Everybody but you,' Tara Hackett says. 'Maybe if you had yourself some sleep you won't be so angry, now would you?'

'I aint angry.'

'Anyone ever told you it's okay to be angry?'

'I aint angry,' Harper says again, 'nothin to be angry about.'

'You gone be angry when the switch flipped on me?'

'They aint gone flip no switch. You're gettin the needle.'

'They already give me needles. I aint afraid to die.' Tara Hackett almost smiles, again. 'Why you here?'

'—I dunno where to go.'

'Go and ask that pretty Mama of yours. She tell you where to go. She knew how to get Herself gone. Good on Her.'

'She's going to Texas cause my daddy sendin Her there.'

'Go with Her—prolly why he sendin Her there. He prolly thinks you follow.'

'It's too hot in Texas.'

'It's too hot everywhere, sweetheart,' Tara Hackett says. 'Get goin, girl.'

'They said we got ten minutes.'

'Nah, you gone. Listen—you don't come here no more, Harper. Get outside, it's summer. Don't be wastin no more time on me. You free girl. You still a whore but free at last.'

Tara Hackett returns the phone to its hook, rises, and the two guards drag her thick limbs back to death row.

I saw on the news that churches from around the county protested at the barbed wire fence lining the prison grounds with signs and candles saying the whole thing was blasphemous to God, killing one of his simple children like that, killing her in the state she was in. But it didn't matter.

Her last meal was a six-piece chicken nuggets meal and a Frosty from Wendy's before she gave some final words. Reporter on the TV said her last statement was short, mumbled through her swollen lips, saying she was real happy she wouldn't be tired no more. The only thing she said about Sister Paul was that she was real sorry she had called her a nigger all those times. But that by killing her they were doing her a favour. Now she would finally have a chance to lay down and rest. Then she said, 'Thanks, thanks Warden'

And I was right you know. She didn't get the chair. They gave her the needle.

Nineteen, Nineteen and Twenty-One

'Thanks,' Harper says when Caro slides Tillie's car against the curb in front of the Harper's daddy's house.

'For what?'

'The ride.'

'I love you,' Caro says, 'I do. I mean it.'

Job stands in the front yard with his battered brown glove on his left hand, tossing a baseball about twenty feet above his head. Launching the ball up into the air, he looks straight into the sun, focusing as the ball falls. He catches it. Doesn't drop it. The ball never touches the ground.

'You shouldn't.'

'I do. And if you left again, if you had to leave, I'd forgive you. I'd be really proud of you if you left. I would,' Caro says quietly.

Harper says nothing.

'Would you forgive me? I don't think Collier would. But would you?'

'For what?' Harper asks.

'If I left—if I never came back.'

'Where we suppose to be if we aint suppose to be here?'

'Would you? Would you forgive me?'

'Do whatever the hell you want, Carolyn,' Harper calls as she steps out of the car and slams the door behind her.

Caro's never been here because it's far from where she lives now and because she finally realized whatever it is I have, whatever it was Collier used to have, is contagious. She calls lots though, at night when she's drunk or during the day when she's sad. Caro writes too if she has the time but sounds like she's awful busy. She sent me some pictures a while ago of her husband and her kids. She married this guy called Matthew who she met at college. He teaches high school math, coaches baseball and looks like what Caro needs, nice honest eyes and an easy going smile. They got two daughters, one called Kathy and one called Lynne. They both look an awful lot like Caro even though Caro thinks they don't. The four of them all live together in Lake Providence, Louisiana—in a cabin on Caro's daddy's farm. Caro's daddy Dennis Naylor who has dicks for brains.

In one of the pictures Caro sent, the girl called Kathy has no hair because Caro said Kathy got real sick right after her third birthday. Caro said she tries not to blame Tillie for giving her grandbaby poison because it's crude to curse someone who has passed, especially when that person is somebody's mother, but she says sometimes she can't help it. The one called Lynne has long dark hair like Caro does. Caro says both girls are wonderful. I'm sure they are.

183

Caro says sometimes she watches her daughters sleep and prays that nothing will ever touch them or harm them or hurt on them. Caro prays that they'll be real strong girls who will always protect each other. Caro says she didn't pray from the time Tillie died to the time when Kathy was born because she had no reason to. 'The sky is empty,' she told me more than once. But Tillie hates that kind of talk and I'm glad that Caro's praying again. Now Caro says she prays for me. I asked her one time if she ever prayed for Collier and she said no. Caro said there wasn't a single reason on earth to pray for Collier. Caro says she only prays for girls who have a chance at being saved but I think Caro forgot about all the girls Collier saved— the ones she saved from having to live. And I figure if Caro could think about it that way—that Collier was the Saint of the little girls who never were—maybe Caro would feel better about everything instead of being mad and hard all the time.

Caro earned the life she got. Caro earned the right to be safe. Caro earned the right to be boring and Caro earned the right to wear gloves to church and to fan herself with a crumpled bulletin and live on her daddy's land. Caro earned the right to go to bed with the same man every night then wake up next to him and him not hit her. She earned the right for a good man to love her and say he would forever. Caro earned the right to be normal and lazy. Caro settled but she earned it. She did. And Caro earned herself a life that was easy. And finally, after giving up on everybody and trying to fix everybody else's shit, she started earning things for herself.

Nineteen, Nineteen and Twenty-One

'Need a favour,' Harper says, tripping up the stairs and counting her breaths.

'It'll cost you,' Job calls from his room.

The stairs shift underneath her feet, rocking back and forth easy like wooden waves.

'Need you—' Harper hiccups, 'need you take me to work real quick.'

Job's head pops through his doorframe and he's smiling real big looking nothing like their daddy and this makes Harper smile too.

'I can drive the car myself?'

'Just a short ways is all. I'll teach—' she hiccups again. 'Cmon, cmon I teach you. I teach you to drive.'

His eyes widen and he jams his feet into shoes without untying them. With his heels hanging over the back of his shoes, he skips down the stairs taking three or four at a time.

'Slow down, gone break your neck,' Harper says, losing her balance and tumbling down the stairs herself as Job rushes through the front door, leaving it open.

He's steady driving down the block towards White's convenience store even though he barely clears the steering wheel. His head and neck strain, his chin pushed upwards trying his best to peer out the windshield.

'Can you see?'

'Nah, well—sorta, I guess,' Job says, squinting.

'It's fine. You don't need to see. Listen to me and I'll tell you when to go. Just listen real careful to me. Listen to me, all right? You hear me, Job?'

'Jesus, I heard you.'

'Take the Lord's name in vain again and I'll slap the shit outta you.'

Twice Harper jerks the wheel away from him to keep the car from hitting something or someone. He cuts the wheel hard, turning into White's parking lot and Harper yanks the keys from the ignition. 'Cmon, I gotta get somethin real quick.'

She buys a pack of Marlboro Lights with the cash Tillie gave her with his body following too close behind her. When they return to the car she sees the can of Skoal tobacco he's swiped.

185

'Shouldn't be stealin,' Harper says, placing a cigarette into her mouth. Biting it too hard, she snaps it in two. 'Shit.' She spits its broken body on the floor.

'Why?'

'Cause, just cause thou shalt not steal and all that,' Harper replies. 'Stealin leads to more sin and more sin always lead to murder.'

'No it don't—Jesus didn't say that.'

'Put your damn seatbelt on.' Harper jams the key into the ignition. 'Jesus Christ, Job—'

'Gimme second.' Job pulls a pinch of tobacco from the can and stuffs it into his bottom lip. It settles into a small bulbous tumor against his gums.

'That's disgustin,' Harper says, lighting a fresh cigarette and rolling down the window.

'You the one who's disgustin.'

'Just, just shut up and cmon already, I'm late.'

It's rough at first, the quick exchanging jolts of accelerating and braking. The worn leather seats crack and splinter under Harper's legs. The backs of her thighs are slick with sweat and slide on the seat with each sharp beat of Job finding his rhythm. Harper closes her eyes and presses her head against the back of the seat. When she opens them, Job is steering with one hand and grabbing for an empty Coke can on the floorboard with the other.

'EyesonaroadJob.' Harper closes her eyes again, taking long pulls of the cigarette to calm her stomach.

'Yours closed,' he says. Somehow he's placed another pinch of tobacco in his lip while he balances the makeshift aluminium spittoon on his leg.

'I aint the one drivin. Pay attention, Chrissake. Cmon, take a left up here.'

The intersection has real narrow lanes like some asphalt horse track. Job spits into the can as the Buick creeps towards the stoplight. He goes to turn left, ignoring his red light, and doesn't see the Ford turning right towards them. Job punches the gas pedal and they heave forward. Harper's head meets the dashboard and she yanks Job back into his seat as he stomps the brake. They come to a quick halt, just inches from the poor prick's fender. Leaning out her window Harper screams, 'Hey asshole, he just a kid is all.'

Harper thrusts her middle finger in the air and snatches Job's Coke can, chucking it at the Ford as it speeds off. Job has tobacco juice running down his chin and his face is real pale as he swallows hard.

'Aw, cmon,' Harper says, leaning over him to open his door and switch on the hazard lights. 'Not in the car.' Cigarette ash falls onto Job's shoulder. He bends over and vomits onto the concrete median. The stench of his puke and scorched rubber and the whiskey burning in her stomach gives in sharp spasms. She swallows vomit and bile back down.

'Yeah, that's right. Get it all out—get the poison out,' Harper says, taking long drags and rubbing his back.

'Sorry.' He leans back into the car and shuts his door with his head bowed in prayer and shame. He won't meet her eyes. For a second, she knows he's praying, or at least trying to. Nobody ever taught him how.

'Coulda killed yourself, hey—you know that?' Harper switches her cigarette from her right hand to her left and gives Job a sharp smack to the back of the head. Just like the one she's always wanted. 'You gotta—Job, listen to me—you gotta keep your eyes on the road. I mean it. Cmon lets switch, let me drive. You want me drive so you can dip like some fuckin cracker?' She flicks the Skoal tin in his lap. 'Hell's wrong with you?'

'No, I'm okay.' His voices cracks and he's making these wet sighs, swallowing tears that haven't come yet. 'You can't drive. Don't want ya to get in trouble like last time and have to go away again.' He still has tobacco juice running in a wet track from his bottom lip to his chin. It settles into a full brown drop, waiting to fall.

Harper places her hand on the back of his head and runs her fingers over what's left of his shortly cropped hair. She takes a drag then flicks the butt out the window. The humidity is heavy on the back of her neck, a sweaty kiss against her shoulders.

'I'm sure.' His tightly gripped fists return to the steering wheel and she can't take her eyes off the mess of his face.

'Dip's horrible for you. You know that? Caro says her uncle had surgery, this skin graft of his gums. You know what that is? It's when doctors scrape and carve out the cancer with a real sharp scalpel.'

'Uncle Henry died drunk with a black lung last year but that aint stopped you none.'

Harper smiles so Job smiles too. She props her feet on the dashboard and the sun beats down on to her legs. And for just a minute, the air doesn't feel as heavy as it should.

'Uncle Henry's a piece of garbage and I'm glad he's dead.'

'You mad you can't drive yourself like Caro do?' Job asks, looking at her.

'Nope.'

'Daddy said it's a good thing you can't drive.'

'I bet he did.'

'But I'm glad you home,' Job says, waiting like he knows something is coming. But nothing ever does. 'I said, I'm glad you came back home.'

'I heard you.'

'You late for work?' he asks. 'Gone get fired now?'

'I can't go to work. I'm sick.'

'I'm sorry.'

'It's fine,' Harper says, 'Get us back home? It aint far, home's close.'

'Sure can.' He rolls his window down, his eyes straining in the sunlight. 'Sure is fuckin hot today.'

'Don't say fuckin, Job. It aint polite.'

'You got more sin in your mouth than the devil do, Harper.'

My biggest sin isn't that I am thirsty and sad and a liar, and it isn't about what Bart found in Her car. My sin is that I am the same I always been and that I never tried to rid the poison in me. I ache for the girls we could have been, Caro and me and Collier, ache for the girls we were too afraid to be. My body could tell you more than my mind or voice ever could. Maybe that's why folks are scared of poison—it's more honest than words or flesh ever could be. All the women I ever known and loved had poison in them. Sometimes it was in their words and sometimes it was in their bodies and their breath, on their tongue and in their pulse. All the women I ever known rotted from the inside out and I figure it's my turn soon.

I'm telling you all this so you remember who I really am and because you have to stop all this. You have to stop calling here because I won't answer. Never. Don't want you to call me ever again, or try and come see me like you did at Christmas, and my birthday, and Her birthday. Stop writing here too. You doing all this garbage because you think you love me, but you don't. You can't love me like you say you do without hating me some. That's okay Job. I want you to. It's okay. It's good. Can't have love without hate. There's not much difference between hating someone and loving someone. Not if you really think about it.

You need to stay gone and save that little girl of yours. You need to think about how even if you got folks, you can still be an orphan. And if you are that orphan you'll spend all your time just waiting to be snatched, waiting to be claimed by something or somebody. And who will claim you if your daddy too scared of you and your Mother too tired to hit you? What then? You need to save that little girl of yours and let her be a little girl. You need to give her a new name, a different name than the one you gave her. You need to change her name from Harper to something that'll give her a chance. Maybe give her a name from the Bible. How about

189

Mary? Or Abigail? That means 'Father Rejoices' in the Bible. I think Abby would be an awful pretty name for a little girl. Or if you don't like Abby, how about Bethany? I like Hannah too. Spelled the same way backwards and forwards so she'd never write it wrong.

Names your folks give you don't mean nothing. Even you— you were supposed to be Joel after our daddy's daddy but our daddy and Her couldn't afford medicine or the shots for birthing. She was dealing with the pain best She could but couldn't talk much sense when you came out. The nurses all took turns holding you and asking Her, 'What's he called, Miss Lucy? What will you call this miracle a yours?' She was so messed up from all the pain and sadness spilling out of Her that She could barely speak. She tried hard to say Joel but all that came out through the slurring was Job. So you were baptised Job. Job—man who weeps. Job the most tempted man that ever lived. A man who never once cursed God even though God took everything away from him and ruined his whole family and his whole life and everything he worked real hard to have. And after all that he still loved God and he still praised God and his name was Job. Job. Job not Joel. Names our folks give us don't mean nothing.

I made a promise to God—I told him that if He saved Her and didn't take Her like He took all the others, I would make sure our family didn't have no more sick girls. I promised God I wouldn't spread any more sick and poison in this family. I am empty and I am barren because I'm in the business of saving little girls. There's a chance a little girl will be born with poison and there's a chance that she'll be born good and pure. But I promised God I wouldn't take that risk because there's always a chance she'll have poison and be dangerous. But some girls don't need to be saved because they don't want to be and they're the most dangerous of all. The girls are damned. They're born poisoned with the sin of their mothers and for those girls, nothing ever starts or stops, everything just is. Caro and me and Collier all had poison but Caro wanted to be saved while Collier didn't. I still don't know what I want but I know for certain I had poison in me long before I laid with Tara Hackett, a murderess. And it was Tara Hackett who taught me that murderesses never start anything. They have no birth, death or resurrection. They just are.

Even now, I still don't know when this all started. Suppose you could say that all of this started when She had me, just a kid having a kid, or maybe this all started when Caro showed up and taught me and Collier how to suck a joint or maybe it started when I helped Collier kill her first little girl before the girl was even a little girl. Or maybe this started when I let a prisoner make me feel nice because I never been able to say no to nothing.

So I guess what I'm saying is I don't really know where or when all of this started but I'm the best liar of us all.

Fifteen, Fifteen and Seventeen

The only place that does it—does it without angry eyes and without questioning the stack of crumpled cash you dump on the desk—is this place called Wyndam or Bedlam or something like that, but Harper never remembers because she doesn't want to. It's three counties to the northwest, hour and fifteen minute drive from Harper's daddy's house if you're driving too fast. The three times before this time, Tommy left Collier out front of the red brick building. He just sat in the front seat of his truck with the windows rolled down yelling, 'Give a shout when you back in town,' after handing her a fistful of twenties then peeling out of the parking lot.

'You want us to come?' Harper asks, watching Collier pitch grey stones towards Donna's house, seeing how close she can get to a window without breaking the glass. She's real good like that. Harper has never seen her wreck a window, never seen her make a small dent or a crack. Collier has good aim and real steady hands that never shake. She never has tremors and her body never seizes because she always tells her body what to do. It works for her. Nobody else does things for her.

'Nah,' Collier says, shaking her head and lobbing another rock towards the house. It falls into a pile of loose gravel, just a couple of feet short of the front door.

Harper and Caro sit in the yellowing bed of brittle grass watching Collier toss rocks. It's a clear day and the blue ridges and dull peaks of the far away mountains are humped endlessly across the cloudless skyline.

'You got same doctor or whatever?'

'Jesus, Caro, I dunno. Aint a reunion. Bet you think they rinsed off same coat hanger they use the other times.' Collier places a cigarette into her mouth and cups her hands around the flame, inhaling when the tip catches.

'That aint funny.' Harper lies onto her back, dead grass pricks invisible holes through her shirt.

'You know, if it was me—'

'Well, it aint, now is it?' Harper says turning to Caro, watching her, wondering what she sees when she looks at Collier.

'Don't worry, Carolyn, won't never be you. You a good Christian gal just like your mama.'

Caro chucks a rock at Collier who dodges it and exhales a mouthful of smoke towards her.

'Whatcha call it?'

'What?' Collier says. She ashes her cigarette and digs into the earth with the toe of her shoe, searching for another rock.

'Whatcha call it? Whatcha call it if it stayed yours?'

'It aint mine. It aint nothin. Just a small knuckle—a knuckle that don't know me.'

'That's a terrible thing to say. If it was me—'

'It aint you,' Harper says.

'They gone bleed out my sin—just an exorcism is all.' Collier places her palm on Caro's forehead and pushes her body to the ground. 'Power of Christ compels you, Sister. Jesus loves you Carolyn Naylor cause Jesus love the little bastards.'

'Shut up,' Caro shouts, kicking at Collier's knees. 'Aint no bastard, you goddam bitch.'

Collier skips then twirls slowly in a circle while giving Caro the finger.

'We'll take you,' Harper says quietly.

'No, you won't. But yall come pick me up if you want.'

'How we gone get there?' Caro asks. 'Where we suppose to get money for a bus ticket?'

'We just—we will.' Harper palms a rock and stands. She tosses the rock with sharp, fine edges, giving it a high arc. With the sun in her eyes, she squints, losing track of its path as it falls.

'Not bad,' Collier says and nudges Caro with her foot. 'Don't pout, Carolyn, I still love you even though you a bastard cause your daddy couldn't stand the sight of you.'

'You're a piece a garbage, Ann-Collier. Aint no bastard cause all I need is Tillie but even if I was, rather be some bastard than a coward who runs away tryin to fix somethin real stupid I done—again. If you ever let one of your girls slither outta you, she be as fuckin stupid and scared as you are. You're a real piece of trash. I'm glad you're doing it again cause some mama you'd be—how could you ever be a mama when yours went and gave you away?'

Collier says nothing. Her eye sockets sink deeper into her skull and her pupils are as silent, dull and dead as lumps of coal. Collier turns from them and walks into her mama's backyard to the sound of their nothing.

'Aint no bastard,' Caro yells the words Tillie tells her all the time, 'aint no bastard and aint no coward neither. There'll never be no little girl I'd bleed.'

Harper sits on her bedroom floor, taking long swigs and tasting Caro's sour lip-gloss on the bottle's mouth. She stares at Her record player and she wonders if the room Collier's in right now—the one that is maybe-sterile with an operating table and metal tools and too-bright lights and doctors who fix fallen women and their mistakes—has music playing. But maybe there's no music, just the soft hum of the air conditioner turned up high as it goes. There could be a muffled chorus of doctor voices from the hallway, talking about her condition, deciding if this careless slut is ever going to learn. Or, maybe the room is real quiet and all Collier can hear is the leak of her own breathing and soon to be bleeding. Harper has never been in a room like that because Caro and Collier are real good sisters who make sure she never has to.

Harper wonders if Collier will look different, if this time she'll be able to see a change in her. If she'll see Collier's hollowness in that empty space where the little girl should have been. But nothing changed the first and second and third time and today is the same. Could be it seemed that nothing had ever changed because Collier is good at smiling when she doesn't want to.

Caro and Harper are late with time lost in mouthfuls and lazy swallows. They dizzy themselves passing the bottle back and forth, promising each other that this sip, no this one—I mean it, this one here—is the last one before they leave for her. Leave to get Collier and bring her back *here*.

'We gotta go.' Harper crawls from the floor to her bed. When she stands, her head spins tight and fast as a top, then slowly unwinds. 'We gotta go. Let me find them keys then we goin.' She searches, stumbling through the house, tripping over mounds of soiled laundry, stacks of old newspapers melding together in damp decay and empty cereal boxes. She punches the microwave open, scraping her knuckles on its broken corner. Her keys sit on its round tray like they sometimes do. Harper pockets the keys and slams the door shut.

She's asleep facedown on the floor with a lit cigarette laced between Her fingers, gnawing a burnt kiss into the carpet. The back of Her eyelet dress is flung open, the zipper's silver teeth an unhinged jaw against Her deep summer skin. Harper takes the cigarette from Her fingers and places it between her own lips, tasting the lipstick branded on the filter and kneels next to Her and slips her hand into the back of Her dress. She's sweating and shivering in the heat. Sketching Her spine, Harper maps each ridge with her fingertip. Harper counts each bone, her hand moving further down Her body. A body that does what She wills it to. Harper presses her face into the back of Her head, kisses Her hair while She moans into the floor.

'Don't worry—won't even know I'm gone. You won't miss me,' Harper whispers into Her mouth as Her eyelids flutter and the muscles of Her face twitch, fighting against Her. A slow smile spreads and She speaks without words or sounds.

Harper pinballs down the hall. Chipped plaster rubs her skin raw as she turns into Job's room. He's sleeping in his crib and this is good. Sleeping means he's safe. He's wearing stained shorts with his skinny arms and legs flung out wide. Lying there on the beige sheet like a fleshy starfish, thirsty on the sand. The ear of his stuffed lamb is shoved into his mouth. He sucks on it as his chest rises and falls. Harper stares at the thin veins of his eyelids and everything's okay because he's sleeping and this is good because sleeping means he's safe. She picks his torn blanket from the floor and swaddles him. Even though it's summer, he needs a blanket because he's just a kid is all.

'Gimme a cigarette,' Caro slurs, slumped against the doorframe.

'Get your own cigarette, moron. Cmon, we gone go.' Harper jams her arms underneath Caro to make her stand straight then drags her body to the living room. 'Shut up, you gone wake them both,' Harper says, propping her against the couch while fishing the car keys from her pocket.

Caro falls, knocking a full ashtray from the arm of the couch onto the floor. 'You a mess, Caro—you can't hold nothin in you. You always gone be like this—damn sloppy, I know it.'

'Itsitsalrightnowsee?' Caro says, nudging Her with her toe. 'She don't need it right now, now do She?'

Harper opens the door and takes a long drag as afternoon sun rushes in. She scrapes Caro off the floor and pushes her through the door. Caro's body doubles, falling onto the broken and busted walkway.

'Walk, Carolyn or I'm gonna punch you in the face. Swear I will—try me.'

'You will not.' Caro sways on the porch like a drunken marionette. 'I'm gone be sick. Why we even goin? Why you tell her we come?'

'Don't be like that,' Harper says, leading Caro to the car. She pushes the shed key into the door lock and the key ring drops to the ground. Harper tries to pick it up but loses her balance and falls. 'Sonuvabitch.'

'Sonuvabitch,' Caro mocks. Harper kicks at the scars on the backs of her knees and Caro tumbles again.

'Shut up. You the worst.'

'You shut up,' Caro laughs.

Harper opens the door of Her Buick. Grey paint peels from its heavy boxed body. Its frame is wide, low to the ground with a short roof—a see-through coffin. Harper pushes Caro into the passenger's seat, shoving her skinny limbs inside and whips the seatbelt across her lap. Caro's knees are bleeding. Flesh buds, bone under skin, open and pucker with pus and blood.

'It's hot, don't.' Caro swats Harper's hands away. Harper spits at Caro and shoves the belt latch into the lock. The belt is strapped to her body, restraining her, protecting her. With the seatbelt tight across her chest, Caro goes real quiet all of a sudden and her eyes begin to shut, like a sick mutt waiting to be put to sleep. A tired old bitch who has surrendered.

Harper forces the door shut and stands in silence, staring at Caro through the thin piece of glass. Harper nearly trips as she climbs over the hood. It's so hot her pores seep whiskey. Nausea slinks up her throat and slides slowly back down again. But Caro's the one who's never been able to hold her liquor. Harper's body is buzzing like she's being touched all over by someone else's skin rubbing against hers in a sweaty friction and it doesn't matter that it's so hot because it's nice and wonderful to be touched is nice and wonderful there's nothing wrong with wanting to feel nice feeling wonderful not many things feel this wonderful.

Sweat coats the back of Harper's legs making her flesh slide against the seat. She is everywhere, everything is Hers so She is everywhere. A dozen cigarette butts stained in bright red lipstick litter the floor with crumpled fast food receipts, an empty sandwich bag that smells of weed, used brown Q-tips, a pair of Job's sneakers with the soles ripped out, a thin brown belt, a dog leash, a stale bag of Fritos, a Gatorade bottle half-full of something that looks like water. A broken and mostly eaten *Fresh Fruit for Rotting Vegetables* cassette hangs from the tape deck with its black film wilting above the ashtray.

Harper winds her handle counter-clockwise and the window creeps down letting a few inches of outside into the car. She tosses Her cigarette out the window and peers through the bug-spattered windshield, squinting hard, trying to blink away her mind. She forces the sun visor's cracked mirror into the roof before she can catch a glimpse of herself. Grabbing a half-smoked cigarette from the floorboard, she lights it then starts thinking you never realize how raw your throat gets until you stop pulling from the pack. One after another doesn't really matter because it's just breathing in and out. You don't think anything of it until it stops because it's when you stop that you start feeling it. You realize how much you ache. And how your mouth tastes like nothing but hot, just-laid asphalt, crumbled bits of fresh tar, playground blacktop at noon. It aches. So you light another.

'Wake up,' Harper yells, forcing the key into the ignition. Inhaling, she flicks the radio on and slowly turns the dial to the left, listening as best she can so she'll pick the right station. *Hot Stuff* fills the car. Caro's still silent with her eyes shut. Harper calls her name three times then screams it twice. After struggling with the key, she starts the engine. She grips the steering wheel just like she's seen Her do a million times. Just like She had when She pulled Harper onto Her lap a long time ago, breathing a sweet reek of morning poison into her ear and saying, 'Your turn now, your turn to learn now, sweetheart.' Harper wraps her fingers around the wheel making two tight fists with skin pulled taut over the sharp peaks of her knuckles. She watches her hands like they belong to someone else. Watches them like they are Her hands.

'We gotta go get Collier so wake up, Caro. We gotta go get Collier. Caro, you dead or somethin?'

Caro says nothing with her eyes still shut.

'Caro, wake up. Cmon now.'

Caro says nothing with her eyes still shut.

Harper ashes her cigarette then gives her a sharp smack across the face. Caro says nothing with her eyes still shut, her cheek already pink. Harper's sweating but she's shivering too because something cold laps at her skin, chewing at her flesh, like always. Collier's communion is honest and pure. It never changes. Her stomach springs into her throat.

'People die like this, Caro.' Harper reaches towards the floor, grabbing the half empty Gatorade bottle. She looks at Caro's face for a long time, thinking about how she'll make a really pretty corpse. Caro is pale and still enough to be one. Harper knows this is the most peaceful Caro has ever felt as she uncaps the bottle and pours it into Caro's face. Caro's eyes burst open and she starts gagging. She leans forward, coughing and choking, her hair hanging in front of her eyes like a slicked veil.

'We gotta go—it's just water now—'

'Aint no water, it's your Mama's shit,' Caro says before a thick jet of earth-coloured vomit spills down her front and on to the floor. She's hacking up sick and Harper's gripping the wheel even tighter, feeling the heart and lungs of the engine underneath her feet. Caro's white t-shirt is see-through, soaked in puke, sticking to her like a second skin.

'You're disgustin.'

'You are, pourin poison in someone's face—'

'I thought it's water,' Harper says, 'I said I thought it's water.'

Caro spits on the floor and then leans back into her seat, breathing like she just ran clear across the state. 'Since when your Mama had a drink a water—never.'

'We late—' Harper rubs her arm against Caro then returns her hands to the steering wheel.

'Not my fault. You had—' Caro wipes her mouth with the back of her hand, '—just much as I did.'

'Yeah but I aint pukin my guts out. People die fallin asleep drunk, Caro, don't you know nothin?'

'I hate Donna Summer so change a station or I'm pukin again.'

'Change a station yourself,' Harper says without a frown or anger or her Mama's hate that lives in her belly. She pats Caro's thigh real soft even though she wants to punch her clean in the mouth.

'Maybe it's a sign,' Caro says, wringing her t-shirt into her lap. 'Maybe we ought not go.'

'Who gone get her then?' Harper revs the engine then slides the automatic gearshift into reverse. The black tab on the dashboard settles onto the white R. She lifts her foot from the brake and they coast backwards into the street. Harper presses the gas then switches to the brake and back again. The car lurches backwards then comes to a quick stop as Harper bounces from one pedal to another. She yanks the handle down into drive and they shoot forward. Caro's now conscious corpse flings back and forth as Harper tries to find her rhythm. The staccato jolts make the steel box and its tires reek of burnt rubber and gasoline. She watches the mailbox disappear in her rearview mirror, its broken bones of wood and tin hidden underneath the back bumper. Luke will have to rebuild it. Again.

'Yaint never gone get no license cause you drive like garbage—drive good as your Mama. And guess what? She drives like shit.' Caro dry heaves until she hacks up yellow bile and red spit on the floor.

'When you gone stop?' Harper pulls the sun visor back down to block the bright shine pouring through the windshield but she punches it shut again when she steals a sight of her own bloated and dripping face. 'I mean Jesus Christ—'

'You shouldn't take the Lord's name in vain so much. You headed to hell as it is.' Caro is breathless, panting heavy, and sucking up every last bit of air in the car like some sweaty thief.

Harper jabs the gas pedal and the acceleration leaps before she pounds the brake, sending Caro's head colliding into the dashboard.

'That hurts. In a funny real funny way. Know what I mean? Do at ever—ever, ever happen to you? Can't feel my face.' Caro wheezes, laughing and with her body desperate to breathe.

'Caro, Caro, you hear me? Aint nobody gone be there for her. Only us.'

Caro laughs and laughs and laughs. She doesn't get it like she should so Harper palms the back of Caro's head and drives it as hard as she can into the dashboard.

'Listen to me—I said nobody, nobody Carolyn, it aint funny—nobody gone be there. We gotta get her.'

Caro's nose is bleeding now and she's groping at her face. Blood runs from her nose to her lips to her chin. Caro touches the stream and then studies her hands carefully, looking at them like she's never seem them before, like maybe they're not even her hands at all. She brushes them against her once-white shirt and she's not laughing anymore. 'It hurts.'

'Burn that shirt when we get back home,' Harper says. 'And get a napkin out the dash, Jesus, Caro—'

'You broke my nose is what you done. Broke my nose—'

'Stop it, aint broke nothin—here, pinch it up here—it'll stop the bleedin. Aint even bleedin that bad. Aint nothin wrong, you just a soak. Here, hold it here—'

'Don't touch me.' Caro wipes her face with a damp bit of her sleeve. 'You hurt me real bad.'

Harper pinches the bridge of Caro's nose to stop the bleeding. Caro winces but lets her and they sit in silence and bleeding for nearly a minute.

'It hurts—'

'Stop movin then. It'll stop once you shut up. Stop talkin. Hold on, there's napkins in the dash like I told you.' Harper squeezes the glove box's lock but it doesn't budge. She punches at it until she splits the skin of three knuckles while Caro screams for her to stop and the latch opens and the door falls open.

'Jesus Christ,' Caro breathes, pulling the bloated ziplock bladder of white pills into her lap. Her pale face is still streaked with blood and her hands shake underneath the weight of the bag. 'We gotta—you gotta toss em. We can't have em. We can't have em—somebody'll think they ours.'

'She, She'll get mad if we touch it. It aint yours. Just leave it,' Harper says.

Caro's face is still leaking, but something richer than blood, deeper and sweeter, black like tar, shiny like an oil slick.

'They aint yours. I said leave em.'

'Fine—let your drunk Mama damn you, moron.'

Harper forces Caro's face into the dash twice more but neither will cry. Caro scowls and shakes the hurt from her face before opening her eyes. 'I don't care. I don't care,' Caro says to no one. 'I don't care how many times you do it. Do whatever you fuckin want to me. I don't care. I don't care what yall do to me anymore.'

'They aint yours,' Harper says, wiping Caro's blood onto her legs. 'Leave em.'

'Gimme one.'

'Shut up.'

Caro rubs her hand across her split face, letting her pulse paint her fingers and palms and wrists and knuckles, and then smears her own blood and Tillie's blood across Harper's lips. 'You did this. This your fault—all of this. I said gimme one.'

Harper picks four before zipping the lip shut. She offers Caro two and they swallow together. Caro shoves the bag back into the dash and kicks the door shut. The latch slides back into place with a near-silent click.

The only things Harper sees are inside the car. She knows Caro's here because Caro's still whining about a broken nose that isn't really broken, screeching and carrying on and complaining echo in the heat between Harper's ears and won't nothing stop. Maybe if Harper could just make her hands do what Her hands do something but maybe everything one day will be fine honest it will be okay but now Caro's drunk face is real pathetic Caro's still wasted like Harper's wasted but not as gone but probably more confused than Caro seeing how she puked up all her drink Caro doesn't want to go and Harper doesn't blame her because Collier's done things to Caro she shouldn't have done but see Caro hasn't known Collier long as Harper so it's different Harper's sure Caro will learn that Collier is a certain way sure Caro will learn Collier is a certain way that's Harper's favourite thing about Collier is that she's different and special and some people call her dirty but it's not dirty it's raw or beautiful or something else like that but never unclean spoiled nothing like that just special Caro is probably jealous of Collier because she aint brave enough to sit on a curb feeling empty being all alone shouldn't no one have to be alone for something like that when it's not their fault it's not Collier's fault if you really think about it's Harper's fault because if Harper had hit Collier hard enough like Collier had asked if Harper had hit Collier hard enough in the right spot Collier wouldn't have had to beg and love on and beg Tommy for the cash and a ride three counties to the northwest hour fifteen minute drive from Harper's daddy's house if you're driving too fast.

'We gotta go.' Harper stares at the wheel. Her limbs are still. 'We real late as it is.'

'We already late,' Caro replies, peering through her window and searching for a witness.

'No, we—we told her, told her we come.'

'No *you*, you—you told her you'd come. Sides, don't matter. She don't want us there—said it herself, but you never fuckin listen.' Caro looks straight into the sun. Right into the center of it with her eyes real open like she's daring God to blind her.

'Don't be stupid.' Harper pulls Caro's face towards her and away from the sun. 'Gone blind yourself, stop lookin at a sun like that. Don't be stupid, you'll get your eyes all scarred up doin that.'

'I'll do what I wanna do.' Caro pushes Harper away.

Harper punches the gas and the tires spin and squeal against the pavement. The stench of burnt rubber fills the car as they barrel forwards.

'She'd do it for us. Honest she would—sometimes she go and do stupid shit but she's special, Caro. She is. She do it for us—'

The speedometer bounces between orange and white numbers, bobbing back and forth while Caro pinches harder at her still bleeding nose.

'If it was you—I'd do it for you. I done it for you, Caro. Why you such a bitch bout it—'

It's only when they hit seventy miles an hour that Harper

forgets Caro is wading ankle deep in her own puke. Harper believes in the things she can see so she believes in the guts of the car its cheap innards its trash she believes in what she can see one time she read a story about a guy who didn't want a tattoo on his back even though he had tattoos all over his body because he could see those but when he finally got one of Jesus on his back even though he couldn't see it his wife whipped him for it lashings across his flesh she really liked that story coasting to ninety through the stop sign not seeing the school bus only seeing the things in her mind instead of knowing she caught the front fender of a school bus a metal kiss and they spin with the tires fighting against the ground the open windows welcoming the outside rot and burnt rubber and Her car hood breathing black smoke car horns blare and curses hang on a gust of wind.

'The fuck's wrong with yall? You tryin kill somebody?'

The bus driver ushers kids to the grassy patch near the Dairy Queen. Backpacks hang heavy on their small frames and Caro squints, her eyes wet with blood and sweat and smoke. The bus driver keeps yelling while pushing a girl wearing a Brownie uniform and saddle shoes with white socks pulled to her kneecaps from the road. He's yelling louder, waving his arms like a fat windmill and more cars come to a halt, creeping towards the stop signs and rubbernecking but don't they know that's how people get killed.

'That little bitch looks like you,' Caro laughs. 'You got a kid we don't know about?'

A fat horsefly swoops through Harper's window and treads above her nose. It circles, taunting her, before fluttering dizzily and then landing on Caro's arm. Harper swipes at Caro's arm and the fly floats in the thick air before escaping through the window that had welcomed it.

'Two pills aint enough,' Caro says, smiling with her teeth painted red. 'Since when two been anythin? Collier's right. You greedy.'

Harper's eyes are far from the car, miles down the road and clear out to the county limits and the wail of Bart's squad car is already ringing in the distance, its looping yowl a shrill promise. Caro's not laughing now because she's mumbling, her lips moving but no words or sounds come out. Harper wonders if she's praying or putting a curse on Collier because maybe it's Caro who's the witch and Harper vomits into her own lap because she knows there won't be anyone to wake Her up when She falls asleep with a burning cigarette in Her hands Her lips nobody to wake Her up nobody to kiss the back of Her head trace their finger along the lines of Her face and back Her body nobody to help Her rise to make sure Job's still breathing he's just a kid is all can't take care of himself nobody to get Collier sitting on that curb three counties over to the northwest hour fifteen minute drive from Harper's daddy's house if you're driving too fast Collier alone sitting alone on that curb with her insides her lips her blood and guts aching something horrible she pukes until her tongue is dry and all she tastes is rust.

Caro turns to Harper who is now the one wiping her mouth with the back of her hand. Caro's gaze is as tired as Harper's mind and Caro isn't smiling because Collier is the one who's good at smiling when she doesn't want to.

'I aint dead—we aint dead, Harper.'

'Not yet,' I say because every day is the hottest day of my life. Everyday I sweat more than the day before. Every day I am a mile further south, a mile closer to hell. And now under the soft hum of the motor's purring lullaby I drive my forehead into the steering wheel as hard as I can, headbutting until my skin Her skin breaks against the brittle and cracked and vomit soaked leather counting each time my skull meets the wheel— eight. No, nine. Nine times. Does it nine times until it doesn't hurt anymore.

Caro wished more than anything else in her whole life that me and her would have died that day. Sometimes on the phone she repeats the same words, says that everything would have been fine if God had let us die instead. But she only talks like that when she drinks and now she only drinks after her kids and man go to bed. It's funny that Caro's the one who's thirsty now. She's never had a taste for nothing, not like me and Collier did. Caro just always wanted to be invited along. Caro only drinks because she's scared—not of dying but of ending up wherever Collier is. Don't matter if it's heaven or if it's hell, Caro is scared she'll see Collier again one day. Now she's the one who's sick and Collier's the one who's dead and I'm the one who's silent.

Some people choose how they die like Collier did, and others just rot until they can't rot no more, like Tillie did, but everyone expires no matter what you do or who you help or whatever goodness you've tricked yourself into believing you done for others. I never really helped no one. I was too lazy and too tired and too drunk on my own anger every day and every night so I killed them all.

Most of the time in my head we're ten and ten and twelve because at ten and ten and twelve Collier's not dead yet and Caro's still a virgin, sort of, Tillie's body is free from the rot God gave her and She's still here. We're all bored all the time but our bodies never stop moving. But now we're not and I am the age Jesus was when he got murdered.

Read the Bible to your girl and give her a new name. Save her or let her be damned. She's not like Caro and me and Collier. She's not one of us. Because Caro and me and Collier are the girls nobody remembers.

Love,

Harper